Seven minutes to go.

"Maybe you'd like to write about why you're here," Ms. Crofford is saying now. I have a feeling she's talking to me, even though she doesn't look right at me; she's too tricky for that. So I start scribbling real fast:

> *I'm here because my dad asked me to come. He thinks I worry too much or something and Larry Casey told him maybe I ought to be more with kids my age. But Larry doesn't know everything. I'd rather be with my dad any day, plus so far this group seems like a waste of time. Like sitting here writing in a notebook is going to make some kind of a difference for pete's sake. Like any of this matters.*

I look up and Ms. Crofford is over on the other side of the room, patting a chubby little blond girl on the back. The girl has the hiccups. I guess I could just sit here now, but for some reason I keep scribbling:

> *I'll tell you what matters. What matters is my dad is dying and nobody is going to do anything about it. They're just going to let him die and then pretend there wasn't anything they could do. It's just one more guy with AIDS and face it he was gay—they might as well let those people kill themselves off anyhow.*

My pen is going all by itself now, it's hot in my hand.

> *And Larry says the doctors are doing all they can. Ha. Doesn't he read the newspapers? Doesn't he ever turn on a television? Nothing but rain rain rain rain rain rain rain—*

Theresa Nelson is also the author of *The Beggars' Ride* and *And One for All.* She lives in Sherman Oaks, California.

EARTHSHINE

a novel by THERESA NELSON

Published by
Bantam Doubleday Dell Books for Young Readers
a division of
Bantam Doubleday Dell Publishing Group, Inc.
1540 Broadway
New York, New York 10036

ISBN: 0-440-21989-2

RL: 5.8

Reprinted by arrangement with Orchard Books

Printed in the United States of America

April 1996

10 9 8 7 6 5 4 3 2 1

OPM

FOR JENNIFER HAMILTON,
in loving memory of her father, Patrick

"There are many who believe that this disease is God's vengeance, but I believe it was sent to teach people how to love and understand and have compassion for each other. I have learned more about love, selflessness, and human understanding from the people I have met in this great adventure in the world of AIDS than I ever did in the cutthroat, competitive world in which I spent my life."

—*Anthony Perkins*

✳

"And he never spoke to them, except it was in parables."
—*Matthew 13:34*

1 ✳

ISAIAH SAYS if you leave L.A. before the morning smog burns off and head out the Five up to Hungry Valley, you can stop at the Miracle Man's for lunch and still make it home before dark.

He says they have this guy there, the one who runs the place, who's like a magician, only better. He knows everything there is to know about oriental herbs and health food and all that, and he can make it taste so good you don't even notice that you're maybe eating seaweed. Vitamins, too, every kind you can think of: A and B and XYZ. You name it, he's got it. Plus, there's this special water that bubbles up right out of the ground, so clean you'll think you dreamed it and chock-full of minerals. The Water of Life, he calls it; one sip and you're turning cartwheels.

And then there are the Dragon Trees. Isaiah says the Man's got them planted in a giant circle, so they're the first thing you see when you drive up: trees like nothing you ever laid eyes on—big ones and little ones and every size in between—all spiky-headed, with leaves like swords. Like the forest of thorns that grew up around the castle in *Sleeping Beauty*, only worse, because they're real.

And that's not all. If you cut these Dragon Trees open, you know what you get?

Dragon's Blood.

"No way," I tell Isaiah, but he says, Absolutely. It's dark and thick and red, like real blood. And it has magic powers.

"Just look in the dictionary," he says, "if you don't believe me."

So I do, and there it is:

Dragon's blood. The sap of the dragon tree, *Dracaena draco*, native to the Canary Islands. Used for medicinal purposes and in the manufacture of certain coloring varnishes; also for photoengraving. Believed by the ancients to have supernatural potency, conferring strength and bravery.

Well, I have to hand it to him. So then I start worrying: what are you supposed to do, *drink* this stuff? But Isaiah says no, it's too powerful for that; it'd kill you, most likely. But the Miracle Man, he takes it, see, and he mixes it with his special herbs or whatever in this secret formula. And then he puts it in these little bottles that cost about fifty dollars each, and you go up there and eat his special health food and drink the Water of Life and buy a little Dragon's Blood. Then first thing every morning you open up that bottle and take a pinch and rub it in your skin: on your elbows, maybe, or behind your ears. And the next thing you know, you're feeling great, better and stronger and braver than you've ever felt before.

But according to Isaiah, that's still not the best part.

"What's the best part?" I ask him.

He gets this far-off look in his eyes and lowers his voice to a whisper. "The best part," he says, "is the Face in the Mountain."

"Whose face?" I ask.

"God's face," he says.

"Give me a break," I tell him.

So then he shows me this article he found in the paper: *Miracle Seekers Flock to Site of Unexplained Phenomenon.*

Well, sure enough, it quotes all these eyewitnesses who swear it's the truth. One day there was nothing up there but this little health-food place, and the next day, *wham!* Here's God's own face staring out of that mountain.

Still I'm not convinced. I mean, this newspaper picture ain't all *that* clear. "Maybe some kid put it up there with spray paint or something," I say.

But Isaiah says, "No sir, no way, just *look* at that, will you? The beard and the mouth and the nose and those *eyes!* No kid could paint eyes like that. No *person* could. And anyway they're not just painted. They're *carved*, can't you see? Carved right into the stone, like Mount Rushmore. Only that took about a hundred years or something, and no telling how many men, chipping away. This only took God *one night!* One day nothing and the next day, *wham!*"

Well, maybe he's got a point. And anyway now there are people coming from all over to see it, crippled people and cancer patients, folks who are too sick to walk, coming to the Hungry Valley in their wheelchairs and on crutches. And they look at God's face and He looks back, and the ones who believe the hardest get cured.

I ask Isaiah why it doesn't work for everybody.

"Miracles can't work for *everybody*," he says. "Otherwise they wouldn't be miracles."

I tell him I don't see why not.

"Well, they just wouldn't, that's all. It'd be like, I don't know, buying soap flakes or something."

Soap flakes?

Sometimes I think I'm starting to understand Isaiah, and then he says something like that.

I just hope he knows what he's talking about, that's all. Because it's a long ways past midnight, nearly three A.M. already, and pretty soon that alarm clock will ring. And then we're out of here, first light.

Isaiah says when it's miracles you're after, it's best to get an early start.

2 ✳

THE REASON we need one, a miracle, I mean, is that my dad and Isaiah's mom are both sick. Bad sick. That's why we got to know each other at all, which we wouldn't have otherwise. See, I'm twelve and Isaiah is only eleven, even though sometimes he acts like he's about ninety, and we go to different schools and all. But a few months ago our folks started sending us to this youth group that their church organized for kids who are living with PWAs, and that's how we met.

PWAs means Persons With AIDS.

The first day I go to the group—this is back last January, in the middle of all that weird rainy weather—it's coming down like crazy. So I splash my way through the parking lot over to the room where we're meeting. Then I go inside, and this lady named Ms. Crofford hands out these brand-new spiral notebooks.

She says we're supposed to write in them for ten minutes.

"Write whatever comes into your head," she tells us.

"You don't have to show it to anybody unless you want to."

Well, she seems pretty nice, and she *looks* fairly intelligent with that frizzy-curly-salt-and-pepper hair and those smiley gray eyes like you see on some teachers, but frankly what she's saying doesn't make a whole lot of sense. I mean, I'm not all that anxious to have her reading my innermost thoughts, but otherwise how's she going to analyze me or whatever?

"Just write what you're feeling right now," she says.

So I write:

Nothing nothing nothing nothing nothing nothing nothing nothing.

That takes up about a minute and a half.

And then she says, "This is a good way to express your emotions, negative as well as positive."

A funny-looking kid with glasses raises his hand when she says that.

"Yes, Isaiah?" she says, and I'm thinking, Isaiah? Like the basketball star? Give me a break. Because this kid is maybe four foot ten, at most.

"Can we cuss then?" he asks her.

"Cuss away," she says, "if that's how you're feeling."

Well, hell, I figure.

Hell hell hell hell hell hell hell hell hell hell hell hell hell.

Okay, now what?

Eight minutes to go.

The rain is coming down harder than ever, streaming down the windows and crashing on the roof. It doesn't know how to rain regular in L.A.; it has to be some big Hollywood production. I mean, seven years of not enough, and now there's way too much. It's all they ever talk about on the news. They're blaming it on some mysterious ocean current out in the Pacific: *El Niño*, they call it—that's "The Child" in Spanish—because it's supposed to start flowing around Christmastime down near South America. Only this year there's something wrong with *El Niño*, nobody knows what exactly. And now that old water baby is moaning and crying and sticking its wet nose way up here in the City of Angels, where it's making all kinds of mischief: flash floods and mud slides and a mess like you wouldn't believe, houses slipping right off their foundations, for crying out loud. Nothing but—

Rain rain rain rain rain rain rain rain rain rain rain rain rain.

Seven minutes to go.

"Maybe you'd like to write about why you're here," Ms. Crofford is saying now. I have a feeling she's talking to me, even though she doesn't look right at me; she's too tricky for that. So I start scribbling real fast:

I'm here because my dad asked me to come. He thinks I worry too much or something and Larry Casey told him maybe I ought to be more with kids my age. But Larry doesn't know everything. I'd rather be with my dad any day, plus so far this group seems like a waste of time. Like sitting here writing in a notebook is going to make some kind of a difference for pete's sake. Like any of this matters.

I look up and Ms. Crofford is over on the other side of the room, patting a chubby little blond girl on the back. The girl has the hiccups. I guess I could just sit here now, but for some reason I keep scribbling:

I'll tell you what matters. What matters is my dad is dying and nobody is going to do anything about it. They're just going to let him die and then pretend there wasn't anything they could do. It's just one more guy with AIDS and face it he was gay—they might as well let those people kill themselves off anyhow.

My pen is going all by itself now, it's hot in my hand.

And Larry says the doctors are doing all they can. Ha. Doesn't he read the newspapers? Doesn't he ever turn on a television? Nothing but rain rain rain rain rain rain rain—

"All right, you can stop now," Ms. Crofford says, but it takes me a minute to make sense of what she's saying because the blood is pumping in my ears and my throat has this big clod in it and my eyebrows are starting to sweat.

So then she has us stand up and stretch and make a circle, joining hands. There are six of us in this middle-school group, and you can tell nobody is too crazy about the idea of holding hands with some stranger, especially with all these germs in their families. But nobody has the nerve to say no, so we do what she asks. And then Ms. Crofford leads us in this prayer, or not a prayer exactly, because she doesn't mention God or anybody, but I don't know what else you'd call it:

"May we open our eyes in friendship,
May we lend our ears in love.

Hand in hand and heart to heart,
Let's be the best we can be."

I guess it could have been worse. For a minute there I was afraid it was going to rhyme.

All the other kids look about the same amount embarrassed as I feel. We let go hands just as quick as it seems polite and try not to make a big deal of wiping them off on our jeans. Then Ms. Crofford has us all sit down again, and we start introducing ourselves.

Besides me (my name is Margery Grace McGranahan, but everybody calls me Slim), there's the baby-faced blond, whose name turns out to be Lorraine (she still lets out a big hiccup every now and again), a tall wispy-mustached guy named Roberto (probably smokes Marlboros and plays out-of-tune guitar), a short bur-headed jock type named Duke (No way, I bet he made it up during that sissy prayer thing), and a bosomy brunette named Suzannah ("Oh, Susanna" you can practically hear the boys singing).

And then there's Isaiah.

We are none of us, with the possible exception of Suzannah, going to win any prizes for pulchritude, as my dad would say, but Isaiah is definitely the weirdest-looking kid I have ever seen. Instead of hair, there is a black knit stocking cap covering his head, pulled so low it hides his eyebrows. Black as a crow's wing that hat is; up against it his skin is too pale, like the skin of a criminal who has been shut up in jail for a long time, away from the sun and fresh air. His chin and cheekbones are like a criminal's, too: they jut out in three sharp points that give his face a sly, triangular look—like a cat's, I'm thinking, or a cat *burglar's*.

But his eyes are weirdest of all. Two huge blackish

brown circles that would be plenty big by themselves but are magnified to double their normal size by a pair of thick-lensed, black-rimmed glasses. "Coke-bottle lenses," the kids at school probably tease him; I bet they call him Four Eyes, too.

Come to think of it, that really is the way his eyes look: two times two, I mean. *Saucer* eyes, like the dogs' eyes in that awful fairy tale about the tinderbox that's always scared me more than all the others put together, don't ask me why. Eyes that are twice as big as they ought to be. Eyes that look too deep and see too much, stuff they don't have any business seeing.

So what are you looking at *me* for, bub? I think at him.

And he shoots me this little half smile that prickles my spine. Like he's *heard*, for crying out loud.

That's Isaiah, giving me the willies, and I've only known him twenty-two minutes.

The rest of this first meeting is pretty tame. Ms. Crofford says she doesn't want us to feel pressured to talk any more than we want to before we're ready.

"Would anybody like to say anything?" she asks, but nobody does. So then she takes us through this peculiar game she calls a "visualization exercise," where we have to close our eyes and breathe deep and imagine ourselves walking down a road and seeing a house and some kind of water and a bear coming for us. And then there's this wall we have to get past somehow, because we want to get to the other side. Turns out it's where we've been going the whole time even if we didn't know it. Well, I don't really see the point, but anyhow my house is sliding off a mud hill, and my water is nothing but rain, and the bear chases me all the way to that wall. But this is the frustrating part: the wall is made of mud, too, so I never do find out what's on the other side. I just keep slipping back and slipping back, and the bear is getting closer, when—thank the Lord—Ms. Crofford says we can go.

3 ✳

MY DAD was the first one to call me Slim. "Skinny" would be more like the truth. Never mind that my middle name is Grace; I am more the hard-angle, sharp-elbow type—sort of spiky looking, Isaiah says, like a Dragon Tree with freckles. But my dad calls me Slim, in this way he has of spinning straw to gold.

His name is Hugh Alan McGranahan the Third, but everybody calls him Mack. He was born in Texas, like me, but he doesn't live there anymore, because he's an actor, the best one you ever saw. One time he was in a Broadway show called *Into the Light*, and he was so good I almost felt sorry for the guy who was supposed to be the main star. I mean, he was working real hard and talking loud and everything, but he might as well have been invisible next to my dad. When Mack McGranahan was on the stage, you just couldn't look at anybody else. But I guess the critics thought you were supposed to, because they said *Into the Light* was terrible. The way Dad tells it, after the reviews the stagehands called it *Into the Truck*. Anyhow it closed, and there weren't enough acting jobs in New York. So he moved out here.

We live up in the Hollywood Hills, just north of Mulholland Drive—not all the way up there with that rich movie gang, but high enough that we can see the mountains from our living room window. When they're there, that is. On a clear day they're so big and beautiful that you'd swear you could hit them with a baseball and a good right arm, but when there's rain or fog or plain old L.A. lung rot, they disappear so completely that you start wondering if you just dreamed them. My dad likes to say that they're not real mountains at all; they're just these really great sets that Steven Spielberg's special-effects people haul in when they feel like working a little movie magic. And it's funny, I know he's only joking, but sometimes I almost believe him. I mean it's just so weird, the way those mountains come and go. And this is Hollywood, after all.

Our house is what's known as a bungalow, which means it's not all that big and doesn't have a regular backyard, just a steep slope with a lot of green stuff growing on it. Deer come and chew on parts of it sometimes, which is hard to imagine in the middle of a city, but you look out the window and there they are, like my dad says, when you least expect them. They are so quiet, we always whisper to each other when they come, so we won't scare them away. Dad shakes his head and puts his finger to his lips, and then even Sister—that's our golden retriever, who doesn't know she's a dog—understands not to bark. There are two babies and a mother with a limp. I worry about that limp. Sometimes after they're gone I notice I've been holding my breath.

Larry Casey—that's my dad's friend, who lives with

us—Larry calls them a nuisance. They eat all the good things in his garden, he says, the newest orange and grapefruit leaves, the rosebuds and also the ivy. But it is so wild and jungly back there, and anyhow there is plenty where that came from, so I figure, what the heck.

The truth is Larry likes the deer, too, even if he won't admit it. He's like a big bear with a beard and all, so he thinks he has to growl. Dad says he learned it growing up on the streets of the Bronx, New York, which is famous for its tough guys. But I have noticed that when the deer come, and all it would take to get rid of them would be one loud "Shoo!" or even just a tap on the window, Larry is the quietest of us all.

We have coyotes, too. Sometimes at night, when you're driving up on Mulholland, you come around a bend in the road, and the headlights catch them in the eyes, and they stand like statues, watching you. They are only the size of medium dogs, mostly, not even as big as Sister, but you would never confuse them with her or any animal that's tame. They're scraggly and scrawny, and they have this wildness hanging all over them that you can almost *smell*, even with the windows rolled up. You feel them watching you, and the hairs on the back of your neck start to frizz, even though at the same exact second you can't help feeling sorry for how hungry they look.

Sometimes when you're lying in bed at night, you can hear them howling. The first time I heard it I was so scared. I thought it was a whole gang of crazy people laughing, devil worshipers or something. I mean, it's not like regular dogs barking, believe me.

"No, honey," my dad told me. "It's just old Wile E.

Coyote and his gang, hollering about how they wish all us roadrunning varmints would go away and give them back their hills."

"*Their* hills?"

"Well, sure. They were here first, you know."

And they'll be here after we're gone, is what he's thinking. He doesn't say it, but my dad and I don't have to say everything out loud to understand each other. We are what he calls kindred spirits.

We don't have words to waste, or time, either one.

My dad caught the virus that causes AIDS before people knew how *not* to catch it, before anybody even knew what it was. It didn't make him sick in the beginning. It hid away inside him for years and years until last summer, when it came on him all at once and nearly finished him on the first pounce. But then he pulled out of it. The sickness went away for a while, leaving him skinny and weak but still here, still cracking jokes and playing with Sister and laughing, even, sitting up with me and Larry on the old green couch in the TV room, watching *In Search of Bigfoot* or *Attack of the Fifty-Foot Woman* and laughing, just like always.

But sometimes I think he's afraid.

The night after that first group meeting, we're sitting there watching the Clippers play the Suns, and all of a sudden he takes my hand and holds it so tight it hurts. And I can just *feel* it; I know he's fighting off something terrible, but I don't know how to help him. He doesn't say a word; he just sits there staring at the television and holding on to my hand like it's some kind of lifeline. Until finally one of the announcers says, "Yes, Johnny, I would say that Manning has proved himself a star in every department, strength-wise, intelligence-wise, and all-around-wise." And then Dad starts laughing. "All-around-wise?" he repeats, looking at me and Larry with such a crazy-happy light in his eyes that we have to laugh, too. *"All-around-wise?"* And he laughs until the tears run down his face, and I know he's all right again.

I live with my dad because I want to, not because I don't like my mom or anything like that. I like her fine. It's just that she worries too much about certain things—like my grades, for one, and my haircut (or lack of a haircut, in her opinion), my posture, my manners, the gaps in my teeth, you name it. She can't help it. She has too much at stake is all; her whole reputation is riding on me. I'm not blaming her. I guess somebody has to push and pull and prod me into shape, or no telling what a good-for-nothing slob I'd turn out to be. But it wears me out sometimes, all the same—all that *molding*. And so it's kind of restful to be out here with my dad and just feel so—accepted, you know? More than accepted—admired—for what I am, who I am, *right now*, not in ten or twelve years, with a lot of work and a little luck and maybe braces and twirling lessons.

I used to live with my mom and that was okay when she was married to what's-his-name, Bob, because we stayed in our house in Texas where I had always lived and I went to my same school. But then they got divorced, and frankly it wasn't much of a surprise. Poor old Bob, I guess he couldn't help it, but he was just so *boring*, you know? I mean, nothing like my dad.

One time I found this yearbook picture of my mom and dad back in high school, both of them all dressed up and smiling at each other, with funny-looking hairdos and crowns on their heads. She kind of laughed and groaned together when I showed it to her. "Lord," she said, "look at us."

"Did you love my daddy?" I asked her. I was just a little kid then and didn't know how dumb this sounded.

I still remember her answer, though, and how her face looked, thinking about it. "Everybody loved your daddy," she said. "He just—stood out, you know? Like lightning on a dark night. I guess we all got struck."

"So why'd you get divorced?"

"Oh, honey." Mom squeezed my shoulders. "We were just too young. We didn't either of us know what we wanted back then—or who we were, even."

Still, when they split up—well, how are you going to follow lightning? With thunder maybe, but not with Bob.

So anyhow Mom and Bob got divorced, too, and then a couple of years later she married Alex, who is the one she's still with. And I guess Alex is okay, but he has to travel a lot in the microchip business. So we were always moving, and I never knew anybody in the new places, and my grades weren't so good, and plus I was missing my dad. So one day, when we had been living in Texarkana for about a month, I just got on a bus. I had enough money saved up from birthdays and vacuuming and such, and I just left. It was in the middle of the sixth grade, and I knew they'd say no if I asked. That's why I didn't.

Mom cried some on the phone when I got here. I felt bad about that.

But Dad said, "Please, Leland, let's try it for a while. Just to give everybody a breather, you know?"

So anyhow that was more than a year ago, and I'm still here, and we're all still breathing, thank goodness. I guess if Mom knew how sick Dad really is, she'd try to make me go back. But I'm not telling, because it's more than just me needing him now; he needs me, too. Anyway I *wouldn't* go, nobody could make me.

I'd like to see them try.

4 ✳

We have this kitchen clock I hate. It has this terrible tick. It's a big black cat with eyes that move and a tail that swings—back and forth and back and forth—this ticking is driving me crazy. I mean, these are not normal clock sounds I'm talking about. This cat ticks louder than a time bomb in an echo chamber.

My old Sleeping Beauty watch is ticking now, too, the one Dad got me at Disneyland when I was eight. I look up from my notebook and check it: seven and a half more minutes of scribbling.

Larry's mother left him this clock in her will, which is pretty creepy right there if you ask me, but Dad says we have to keep it. What makes it worse is this stupid clock song that keeps running through my head, the one about the old man who dies when his clock stops ticking. That song has always made me nervous.

Ms. Crofford is walking around the room, pausing to pat shoulders and say encouraging words to anybody who's just sitting there. I pick up my pen again before she gets to me.

> *Last night I woke up and heard my dad coughing that way he does when he's trying not to make any noise. I didn't want him to know I was awake because he'd only feel worse, so I just lay there. And then I heard Larry in the kitchen, probably he was making that herb tea Dad is so sick of. And I guess it helped some because after a while the coughing stopped. But I never did get back to sleep, I kept hearing the ticking cat and that stupid clock song even over the sound of the rain. I mean, who would teach a little kid a song like that, I was only in third grade I think. That was the same year that—*

"All right," Ms. Crofford says. "You can stop writing now."

It's weird, but I don't want to in a way. I was just getting warmed up.

But anyway we all get out of our chairs, which are set up in a circle this week, and we stretch and do that prayer thing, staring at our shoes the whole time. After that we sit again, and Ms. Crofford makes small talk for a while: What a pretty belt, Lorraine, and, Wasn't that something, that big mud slide in Coldwater Canyon? and, How about those Lakers, five in a row!

And then she gets down to business.

"So tell us, Roberto, how are things going with your brother home from the hospital?"

Oh, Lord, here we go. So we're all supposed to be best friends now, ready for secret telling?

Roberto doesn't look too thrilled with the idea either. He's slumped low in his seat, pulling on his tiny little mustache hairs.

20

"Okay," he says.

Ms. Crofford smiles. "Wonderful. I know you're glad to have him back. Is it any different this time?"

Roberto thinks that over awhile. "He sleeps a lot," he says finally.

"That's good." Ms. Crofford nods encouragingly. "That's what he needs. But I guess you have to remember to be quiet, don't you? Is that hard sometimes?"

Roberto shrugs and slumps a little lower in his chair. I try to imagine him at home, whooping and hollering through the house, banging a basketball against the wall, yelling, "I'll get it!" when the phone rings—

Somehow I can't see it.

Now Ms. Crofford is smiling at Duke. "And how are things at your house, Harold? Is your dad feeling any better this week?"

Harold? Poor Duke, he turns about forty shades of red. But you got to give him credit. He sits up as tall as he can manage and says, "Yes, ma'am, he's just fine," like this whole thing is a mistake, after all; he really ought to be over at the Weight Lifters' Club or maybe out chopping some wood.

Well, it goes on like this for a while, Ms. Crofford nudging and tugging at us real easy, trying to work her way in, nothing we can't handle. Lorraine is over her hiccups and manages to nod yes to everything, whether it makes sense or not. I pretty much just shake my head no. And Oh Suzannah changes the subject completely and talks about this dress her sister is getting for her senior prom; she's stumped between purple and black.

And then there's Isaiah.

The rest of us are just sitting here trying to act like we

care about this dress dilemma when all of a sudden he blurts out, "Mr. H. B. Goldman on channel three says death is a physical impossibility!"

We all just stare at him. Say *what?*

He nods his black-hatted head. "Oh, yes," he goes on in a rush, "the scientists have proved it, but they don't dare tell because of all the lobbies."

"L-lobbies?" Ms. Crofford, who never stutters, stutters. "What lobbies would those be, Isaiah?"

"Well, the funeral parlors, first. You know they'd be hurting. And then the people who make guns and weapons. And of course that would pretty much wipe out the army and the navy. And we wouldn't need doctors or hospitals, neither one, or the companies that make all the medicine or the schools that teach 'em how to make it or the sad song-writers or the depressing moviemakers or—"

"What are you *talking* about?"

Now everybody is looking at me. I didn't intend to speak up, but this is getting ridiculous.

Isaiah leans in, peering deep with his saucer eyes. "I'm talking about death," he says. "How it's all made up by the ones with the money. The ones *in charge*, you know?"

"Well, Isaiah, that's an interesting idea," Ms. Crofford begins. Her tone tries to soothe, like cool water on a burn.

For some reason that just irritates me more.

"Shoot," I mutter, "that's the silliest thing I ever heard."

"You mean, like a conspiracy?" Lorraine's voice is hardly more than a whisper; her pudgy face is going all pink.

"You got it," says Isaiah. "Like the biggest conspiracy there ever was. Been going on as long as there's been people to fool."

"Well, that's *one* way of looking at it," Ms. Crofford says, "but maybe what you're trying to say is that a person's *spirit* can never die, right, Isaiah?"

"No, ma'am," he says. "I'm saying that he never dies at all. He just *thinks* he's dead, you see. He gets wore out from hearing it preached so much till finally he believes it himself."

"Lot of ignorant people out at Forest Lawn, lying there *thinking* they're dead." This in a low voice from Roberto, who appears to be speaking directly to his belt buckle. I look at him, approving; at least somebody around here has some sense.

Ms. Crofford looks like she wants to smile at that herself, but I guess her manners are too good. Or maybe she read in some book that you're supposed to let crazy people say whatever they want, because she lets the wild talk go on for a while before she takes over again. "Well," she says for the third time straight, "I guess this gives us a lot to think about, doesn't it? And now if you'll all just take a deep breath and close your eyes, we'll imagine ourselves on that road again. . . ."

And she's off with the house and the bear and the wall, only this time with some extras thrown in: people in the house and supper cooking and a boat that can take you away. And I'm trying to concentrate, but all the time I'm thinking about this goofball conspiracy theory. I know I shouldn't care what some weird kid says, but I just can't help it. I keep seeing Lorraine with her pudding face shining, wanting to believe that people don't die, and it makes me want to shake somebody.

I can't stand lies, is all.

5 ✳

OUR FAVORITE old movie—my dad's and mine, and Larry's, too, I guess, and even our dog Sister's—is *The Wizard of Oz*. Only we call it *Boz*, because when I was a real little kid, I thought that's what they were saying: "The Wizarda Boz," get it? My dad gave me the videotape for Christmas one year, and I would ask him to play it over and over again. "Wanna watch *Boz*," I would say, even though I was scared to death of the Wicked Witch and the Talking Trees and the Flying Monkeys—them most of all, for some reason. "Hold you, honey," I would beg my dad then, because that was what he would always say to me when I was afraid: "Do you want me to hold you, honey?" And then I would climb in his lap, and he would keep me safe until Dorothy finally made it back to Kansas.

He never will say that he's sick. A couple of days after that second group meeting, the phone rings, and Larry answers it and then hands it to Dad. "It's David Windsor," he says, looking worried.

David Windsor is my dad's agent.

"Hello, David? Well, I'm just fine, thanks. How are you?

Oh, sure, sure. . . . You mean *today* at four? Well, sure, I guess I could make that. . . . That's in Burbank, isn't it? All right then, tell them I'll be there!"

When he hangs up, he's smiling that million-dollar smile of his. "An audition," he says, "for a pilot."

A pilot is a test episode of a brand-new TV series, which is what all actors out here hope for.

"Wow," I say.

"Today?" says Larry.

Dad nods happily. "It's a last-minute replacement deal. David says the guy they hired first was too low-key, so the director—you remember Will Young, I worked with him years ago in all those crazy musicals back in Houston? Anyway he asked for me."

"Great, Dad," I say. I'm really glad to see him so excited, even though I can't help feeling nervous at the same time. Not that he hasn't ever had an audition like this; before he got sick, he was always trying out for pilots and even came close to getting a couple. But now—well, the auditions just haven't been coming up like they used to. Nobody's really said it's because he doesn't look the same, but I know that's what it is, I mean, what with all the weight he's lost. Plus, some of the medicine he's had to take has made a lot of his hair fall out, and he's got these brownish red splotches on his face. He calls them his beauty marks, but they're a kind of cancer really—Kaposi's sarcoma—lots of PWAs have them.

So anyhow it's been a while. And now the way my dad's smiling—well, I just couldn't stand for him to be disappointed, that's all.

I know Larry's thinking the same thing, even while he's saying, "Great," just like me, and patting him on the back.

But Dad sees right through us. "Don't worry," he says, and his eyes are dancing. "I'll just call the Max Factor emergency number and have them send over a couple cases of that industrial-strength Tan Number Two. And maybe a trowel."

So that gets us laughing and kind of in the right spirit, you know? Like it's all just a big game, really, and only the playing matters.

"What do you think, Sister," he says to the dog, "the polka-dot bow tie or Rootie Kazootie?" And he points to this crazy beanie hat with a propeller on top that he's had ever since he was a kid; he swears it brings him good luck.

"Woof," says Sister.

"Both?" says Dad, raising his eyebrows. "Well, I guess you're right. Better not take any chances." He puts on the whole shebang and turns to me. "How's that?"

"Perfect," I tell him, collapsing in giggles. He looks like a blue-eyed helicopter.

"Just as long as this isn't *Hamlet* you're trying out for," says Larry, shaking his head.

"Of course not," says Dad. He gives his propeller a twirl. "It's *Macbeth*."

❋

LARRY takes him over to Burbank in his little red Toyota. Dad's been having some trouble with his eyes lately, so it's better if he doesn't drive.

"We'll be right back, girls," he calls to me and Sister. It's raining again, naturally, so we're standing on the porch and watching as they pull out of the driveway. "Remember, no worrying allowed!"

"No worrying," I repeat, waving back.

26

He's always telling me not to worry; he says it doesn't change anything, it only makes your stomach hurt. But sometimes I just can't help it. I start thinking that if I worry about something hard enough, then maybe it won't happen.

Still, I guess I promised. So I go back inside and try to do my homework instead, even though it's kind of hard to concentrate with Sister looking so mournful over there at the front window, staring out after the car. It kills her when Dad leaves even for five minutes. I guess it's hard on dogs, not understanding English all that well—you know, words like "I'll be back." I mean, as far as they're concerned, once you walk out that door, you're just gone, period. So after a while I give up on multiplying decimals and call to her: "Hey, Sister, wanna watch *Boz*?"

"Woof," she says, bounding over to the television.

Boz she knows.

✳

WE'RE JUST about to the Flying Monkeys, and I'm starting to get that old queasy feeling in my stomach, when I hear the car pulling up outside.

"Hello, girls!" Dad's smile is just as bright as ever when he walks through the door. Sister jumps all over him, of course, and he scratches her behind the ears and says, "Yes, dear, I missed you, too."

"How'd it go?" I ask. I'm careful to keep my voice real casual, like it doesn't matter one way or the other.

"Fine," he says, "just fine."

Oh, Lord. He didn't get it.

"There were only two of us there," he goes on cheerfully, not looking at me as he takes off his raincoat and hangs it in the hall closet. "Just me and Charlie O'Donnell.

Can you believe it? I haven't seen him since New York. He looks great. Of course, he's a completely different type. I can see how they might want to go that way."

He's not sick, you mean. Well, hell.

Larry is still standing just inside the door on the mat, going through this big act of wiping invisible mud off his shoes. "Who wants meat loaf?" he asks now, louder than he has to. "They had that sausage with the extra sage at Alpha Beta. . . ."

Feeding people is Larry's answer to all the sorrows of life.

"Sounds wonderful," says Dad. "How can I help?" And he loosens his polka-dot tie and follows Larry into the kitchen.

I don't know what he's done with the propeller hat.

✳

THAT NIGHT I have the roach dream. The one where I am standing in front of the fireplace in my bare feet, and I poke my head inside and think, Look at all those shiny black coals in there. Only that's when they start to *move*. So I run for the bug spray, but I can't find it anywhere, and I have to settle for Windex. I start spraying the roaches with that, and of course they don't die, they just run every which way. So then I look for a shoe, and there is a whole row of them lined up by the back door: Dad's soft brown slippers and Larry's good Loafers and my own Nikes, looking as new as they did when school started way last September. And first I grab one of mine, but then I think about the roach juice and decide, well, no. And then I see that I've overlooked a pair of beat-up fishing boots that I thought Dad had left in Texas. He hasn't worn them in years, and anyway how's he going to know if I don't tell? So I take one of those and start flailing away: *crunch, splat, crunch, smush, crunch, crunch, crunch!* And I'm getting them pretty good; I'm *winning* is the thing, but there are plenty more to go, and I'm still hard at it when I wake up in a sweat.

And the rain is raining and the cat clock is ticking and my dad is coughing again.

6 ✳

THE NEXT DAY the rain lets up some, but in the afternoon Larry says Dad's not breathing right; we'd better take him to the hospital.

My dad tries to talk him out of it. "I'm fine," he says in between wheezes, and he winks at me. "Just fine, all-around-wise."

He hates hospitals, is the thing.

But Larry won't listen. He says we're taking him.

Actually, what he says is "*I'm* taking him," but I'm not about to let them go without me.

Not that it makes much difference. Once we get there, they won't let me in the room anyway. So I end up waiting outside in this drippy little patch of gravel and potted plants that passes for a garden, which makes me want to yell at somebody except I know it won't get me anywhere but sent back home.

So I'm just standing there staring up at a hundred blank windows in a brick wall, trying to figure out the only one that matters to me, when this voice behind me makes me jump:

"Hey, Slim, is that you?"

I wheel around, and I'll be dogged if it isn't the mad scientist, Old Saucer Eyes himself.

"Lord," I say, "you like to scared me to death."

"Sorry." He grins, looking not sorry at all. "I thought it was you." Then his face changes, and he says, "So who're you here for, your daddy?"

I shrug and kick at the gravel. It leaves chalky white smudges on my shoes.

"I'm here for my mama," he says. "Just a checkup."

I don't know what to say to that, so I don't say anything.

"Old Man Bones says she's his prize patient," he goes on, looking real cocky. Like *he* has something to do with it. "Says he might have to retire if she keeps up like this."

I try a mind-reading test. Go away, I think at him.

The test is a failure. Professor Marvel doesn't budge.

"That's what I call the doctor," he's saying now, "Old Man Bones. That ain't his real name. It's Bohens. Alfred P. Bohens, M.D. But you got to loosen him up a little, you know what I mean? Got a face like Darth Vader till you get him to smiling. Then he's okay."

I can feel his big eyes on me, wanting to get inside my head with their X-ray vision, and I know it's my turn to talk. But I'm still wondering which window is my dad's, and all I can manage is another shrug.

It seems to suit him fine.

"I'm Isaiah, remember? Isaiah Dodd."

"I remember."

"My mama knows your daddy. Did you know that?"

I shake my head; this is news to me.

"Oh, yeah," he goes on. "From church and visitation and all. She asked me who goes to the group, and when I said you, she said, '*Oh*, yes, that must be Mr. Mack's daughter. You remember, him and his friend Mr. Casey brought us soup and magazines all those times when I was sick, and that word game'—what-do-you-call-it, Percaffrey or Snerquagly or something."

"Perquackey," I say.

"*That's* it!" Isaiah is beaming now, like he's won a contest. He looks down at his own hands and seems surprised to find an aluminum cylinder there. He holds it out. "You want a Pringle, Slim?"

"No, thanks."

"Come on, take one. Got the crisp you love to crunch."

"I'm not hungry."

Isaiah shakes his head. "Aw, man, tell the truth. You're thin like me. Bet you're hungry all the time."

"No," I say, and now I'm starting to get steamed, "I'm not."

Isaiah only chuckles and takes out a chip, and then he commences to wave it under my nose like he's a snake charmer with some kind of magic flute. "Sure you are. Listen to your stomach growl. 'Feed me, Slim—I'm starving down here!' "

I've had enough. "Look, I'm not hungry, okay? I don't want a potato chip. I don't want to hear about Dr. Bones or Jones or whoever he is. I just want to stand here till they say I can go back in, if that's all right with you; I just want to mind my own business."

It gets real quiet now. For one second, two seconds, maybe even three, there's no sound but the traffic passing in the distance: *whush, whush, whush.* Isaiah's grin fades, and he drops the chip back into the cylinder. "Okay," he says. "Sorry."

And he looks *so* sorry that I wish I had kept my mouth closed, after all. But it's too late now, so I just stand there— since that's what I said I wanted to do—stand there like a jerk, choking back this cloddy feeling that's crowding into my throat again.

"It's all right," he says gently, like he's back to reading my thoughts. "Sometimes on their bad days, you don't want nobody messing with you." He walks away then, up through the little gate and onto the sidewalk that leads back into the waiting room. And then, just when I think I've seen the last of him, he turns around and comes back and puts the Pringles on the gravel beside me. "Maybe you'll feel different later," he says, and then he's gone for real.

7 *

FOR REAL, maybe, but not for long. Larry comes out to the garden finally, looking worried and tired, though he's trying not to show it. What's the matter, how's Dad, can I see him now? I ask, and he says, No, they still won't let me, but he's better, he's resting, he wants Larry and me to go home and get something to eat. And I don't want to go, but I don't know what else to do. And when we get there, we find a message on the answering machine:

"Hello, Mr. Casey? This is Angelina Dodd from church. Isaiah tells me he saw your—he saw Margery Grace over at the hospital. And I got to thinking, well, why doesn't she just come on over here for tonight? I mean, while her daddy is laid up and all, and you probably wanting to be down there. It'd be our pleasure. Isaiah would enjoy the company, and I'm feeling real good lately. Matter of fact, there's this big pot of stew on the stove right now. I'm sure the two of us could never—"

The message cuts off there, but I'm already shaking my head.

"No way."

And I figure that's the end of it, but Larry has other ideas. "Well now, hold on a minute, Slim. The Dodds are nice people and—"

"*No way*, Larry. That kid is weird, okay? I'm not going over there."

"You mean Isaiah? Oh, come on, there's nothing wrong with Isaiah. Look, let's just think about this for a minute, can we? It might not be such a bad idea—I mean, just for tonight. I'd really like to go back and check on Mack, and I can't have you wandering around that garden in the middle of the night—"

"So go back if you want to. I'll be fine. I'm not a baby. I can stay here by myself."

"Nobody said you were a baby, Slim. I'd just rather not leave you here alone, that's all, not in this crazy town. Look, it's not so much to ask, is it? Isaiah's a good kid if you just give him half a chance. And I know you'll like Angelina— she's terrific."

I don't care how terrific she is, I'm about to say. Her son has X-ray vision, and he lies.

But two things stop me.

Number one: that dang can of Pringles.

Number two: Larry's socks don't match.

I'm standing here all mad and stubborn, staring at the floor, and I happen to notice that he's got on one sock that's just regular brown and one that's an old green-and-navy argyle, with a hole coming in the heel. Which maybe wouldn't seem like a big deal with most people; I mean, if it were Dad, I wouldn't think twice about it. But Larry is such a *careful* kind of person, it can drive you crazy sometimes. Dad's always teasing him about it—how his shirts have to be pressed so neatly and his shoes lined up just so in his closet and even his dollar bills all facing the same direction in his wallet. So if his socks don't match, well, it *means* something, that's all. And I think back to earlier, him doing forty things at once—tearing around the place, trying to get dressed and call the doctor and steam up the house with the teakettle and the shower going full blast, so that Dad could breathe easier—and I get this sinking feeling in my chest.

Shoot. Why'd I have to see those socks anyhow?

So I find myself sighing and saying, "All right already, I'll go."

Larry just looks at me for a minute, kind of surprised. As if he's thinking, Well, that was easy. What did I say right for a change? And then he clears his throat like he's embarrassed or something and says, "Thanks, Slim." Says it in that gruff old bear growl of his and turns away real quick—before I can change my mind, maybe—and goes to look up the Dodds' number.

✶

THE NEXT THING I know, we're driving over to this old-fashioned apartment building in the middle of West Hollywood—palm trees out in front and peeling pink stucco and all, like something out of one of those old fifties B movies that Dad loves—and we're climbing up the steps to 4-C.

"Will it be just the two of them?" I ask, dreading every minute. "I mean, is there a *Mr.* Dodd, or what?"

"No," says Larry. "He died a few months ago."

The news makes me sick to my stomach. "You mean Isaiah's dad is—was he a PWA, too?"

Larry nods. "But they didn't know until after."

After what? I'm about to say, but before I can open my mouth the door flies open, and Isaiah himself is standing there, smiling.

"Hey, Slim, glad you could come," he says, and then, "Hey, Mr. Casey, how you been?"

"Fine, Isaiah. It's good to see you."

"Hey, Mama! They're here!"

My throat goes tight, bracing for the introductions. Seems like I still get nervous around sick people, except for my dad; I just feel embarrassed someway. I don't know, I guess I'm afraid they'll think I'm stuck up, too proud of my good health, maybe. Well, you're here now, I tell myself, so shape up and be polite, you got that? It's just for one night. You can stand anything for that long—

And then Isaiah's mother walks in the room.

I don't know what I was expecting Angelina Dodd to look like. Skinny and pale, I guess, with her skin all splotched like Dad's. But what I'm seeing instead is this big beautiful woman in a flowing flowery dress, with a blue baseball cap on her head and a shiny white star in the middle of the cap and under that a smile so bright it could save you on your electric bill. A queen is what she looks like, or a star like the one on her cap: a big bright shiny movie-star mother, that's what Isaiah's got.

And she's going to have a baby.

"Hello, Mr. Casey, how nice to see you again!" she's saying, shaking hands. "And this must be Margery Grace. Why, you're just as pretty as your daddy said!"

"You're supposed to call her Slim, Mama," Isaiah tells her. Probably he's thinking that's why I'm still not saying anything.

But that's not it at all; it's just I'm stone-mouthed with surprise.

"Well, Slim, you come on in the living room and sit down, honey. You, too, Mr. Casey. Can I get you all something to drink? Dinner's ready just as soon as you're ready for it. I hope you like stew!"

"Yes, ma'am," I manage at last. "I like it just fine."

Larry says it smells wonderful—which it does—but he has to go; he wants to get back to the hospital. So they shake hands again and say, Thanks so much, and, It's our pleasure, and, Give my best to Mr. Mack. And then he's gone and I'm still sitting here feeling kind of dazed, wondering what am I supposed to do next, and do they let PWAs have babies, and was my dad able to eat any supper?

When all of a sudden a man's voice comes out of nowhere.

"What's your name?" he asks.

"Whaa—?" I wheel around, looking for whoever it is that's talking.

But there's nobody there.

Isaiah just about passes out laughing. "It's just our my— It's just our my—"

"It's just our myna bird, honey," Mrs. Dodd finishes for him. "See there?" And she points across the room to a cage I haven't noticed up to now; it's half-covered by the fronds of a huge potted palm that is trying to take over the world. Sure enough, inside the cage is a yellow-beaked bird with glossy black feathers, speckled with white on the wing tips. It's walking restlessly across its perch, taking slow steps to the left and then scooting right back again, looking at me all the time.

"But that didn't sound like a *bird's* voice," I say. "It sounded like a real per—"

"What's your name?" he says again, and I just about drop my teeth. I could swear this voice belongs to a full-grown man, but there's no doubt where it's coming from this time.

"You gotta be kidding me," I mutter, walking over and looking in the cage. "That's the weirdest thing I ever—"

"What's your name?" he asks once more. This bird has a one-track mind.

"My name's Slim," I answer. "What's *your* name, bird?"

He looks at me sideways. "What's it to ya?"

I am not making this up.

Well, Isaiah is practically rolling around now, he's laughing so hard, but his mom says, "His name is Gabriel, honey, and I apologize for his bad manners. That's one of his favorite routines, for some reason. We can't figure out how he knows to do it every time a new person walks in the door."

"That's all right," I say, though I'm blushing like crazy. "He's a real smart bird."

She smiles. "Better than a watchdog, isn't that right, Isaiah?"

She gives him a look, and he starts pulling himself together. "Yes, ma'am, old Gabriel, he's something else. One time a burglar broke in here while Mama and me were sleeping. And what woke us up wasn't the crook at all—it was Gabe saying, 'What's your name?' Poor guy must've thought a ghost was after him, 'cause by the time Mama came in to check, he was long gone. Never took a single thing, just beat it on out of here and left the door wide open, probably halfway to Alaska by now."

Isaiah pauses for breath and grins at me. "Old Gabe, he's a watchbird, get it?"

Good Lord. I'd never believe it if his sweet-faced mom wasn't sitting here nodding. She doesn't seem like the type to fib, and anyway I guess you could say I've heard the evidence with my own ears. The bird's side of the story, so to speak.

"That's amazing," I say, speaking to the lady. "So what else can he say?"

She chuckles and shakes her head. "We never know what and we never know when. Sometimes he pouts and won't say a word for weeks. Other times he won't shut up: 'Clean my cage' and 'That's not funny' and—"

"Dance with me, Angelina!" This is Gabriel himself, which makes us all laugh.

Then I sit down beside Mrs. Dodd again and ask, "So who taught him to talk? Was it you?"

There's a pause in the room, and right away I know that I've asked the wrong question. For a moment the only sound is a soft ruffling from the cage, where Gabriel is preening his wings.

For once, Isaiah won't look me in the eyes.

But then his mother is smiling as kindly as before. "No, sweetheart," she says. "It wasn't me that taught him. It was Isaiah's daddy."

"Oh," I say, trying to sound like somebody at a tea party who's just been told lemon, not milk. Like it's no big deal, I mean, since that's the way the lady seems to want me to take it. Just, "Oh," I say, "I see."

But the truth is I'm dying inside. And while she's still

smiling and excusing herself to go into the kitchen and check on the stew, I'm thinking, Well, shoot, Slim, what'd you have to go and ask *that* for? You heard it yourself— that was a grown *man's* voice coming out of that bird. Who'd you think he learned it from, Tinker Bell?

I don't know where to put my eyes.

Isaiah's sitting across from me, fiddling with one of those cheesy little games where you try to get the metal balls to roll in the right spots. He's got it up close to his glasses, concentrating till he's almost cross-eyed, like his whole life depends on the outcome.

Seems like he looked younger five minutes ago.

"Those things drive me crazy," I say. Just to say something. Anything.

He stares at me blankly for a moment, then puts the game down and walks over to Gabriel's cage. And stands there, with his back to me.

"Say, 'Hello, Isaiah,' " he says softly.

"Hello, Isaiah," says the bird. In the disappeared dad's voice, I guess.

And I'm opening my mouth to say, "That's great, Isaiah, that's sure one smart bird," when he turns around.

"Mr. H. B. Goldman on channel three says death is a physical impossibility," he says, and he's looking deep into me with those eyes, as if he's expecting some objection.

But I don't—can't—say a word. So then he goes on:

"It's not how you think it's going to be. It's more like— like he's just out of town, you know?"

I nod slowly, not knowing at all.

"He was lucky in some ways. He didn't have to be sick for a long time. Mama says he couldn't have stood that." Isaiah is speaking to me gently now, like before with the

Pringles can—as if I'm the one who needs comfort. "He never found out that she had it, too. Or about the baby coming either."

Oh, Lord, I think, *the baby!* And I can't keep from asking, "Is the baby—all right?"

Isaiah shakes his head. "They don't know for sure. Sometimes the babies get it, sometimes no. They'll have to be real careful when it's time for her to get born. But so far everything looks okay. So far Old Man Bones says she's got a real good chance."

"You know it's a girl?"

"A sister. They checked already." Isaiah smiles a little at that. "We don't know her name yet, but we're thinking."

"Isaiah! Slim! Supper's on the table!"

We're halfway to the kitchen when Gabriel pipes up again. "Hello, Isaiah," he says.

Isaiah looks at me, explaining. "He's good at hello—my dad worked on hello for a long time." He pauses a second, and then adds quietly, "He just never got around to good-bye."

8 ✳

What could Isaiah be writing so fast and furious in his notebook? Is it about his dad or his mom or both? Or the baby maybe. No wonder he thinks there's a conspiracy—I mean how can they stand not knowing if the baby will be all right? I don't know, everything's different now that I've seen them at home. Sure they're nice people like Larry said but that's just the trouble. There's my dad still in the hospital and now here's this whole other family to worry about. Why'd I ever go over there anyway?

I look across the room at Isaiah, and he feels me looking right away and lifts his face to shoot me a smile. I kind of nod back, but I don't get it. How can he be smiling with his mama sick and this baby coming and his daddy dead just last October?

The other night after the stew we're sitting there watching TV and all of a sudden Mrs. Dodd puts her hand on her stomach and smiles and says, Oh my, that was a good one. And Isaiah says, Is the baby kicking? High kicking, she says, and then Isaiah asks me if I want to put my hand there so I can feel. Well I don't really want to but Mrs.

Dodd says, Sure go ahead, and it seems like bad manners to say no so I do it. And it's the weirdest thing, first there's nothing and then this little warm thud comes rolling up under my fingers. I mean there's a real kid in there kicking at me and now I can't ever forget her whether I want to or not.

There's still another couple of minutes to go on the scribbling time, but that's all I can think of so I put down my pen and just sit here looking around and feeling disgusted. What's the idea putting all these hard-luck cases in one room anyhow? I wonder. By ourselves we're already plenty depressing enough, but together we're like one of those disaster specials on the five-o'clock news—not just me and Isaiah but Lorraine over there chewing on her fingernails and Duke filling up his notebook with skeletons on motorcycles and Oh Suzannah trying to get Roberto to look at her but he won't, he's got his eyes closed and his chin on his chest, right on top of his "Life Sucks and Then You Die" T-shirt. I guess it's supposed to help us somehow, seeing how miserable everybody else is, too, but frankly I have my doubts about that. It's too much like that old story—you know, the one about the man with no shoes who feels so sorry for himself until he meets the poor guy with no feet? I mean, sure there's a lesson there somewhere, but it's never seemed to me like the ideal way to cheer a person up, that's all.

Maybe it's just this rain getting me down. I can't believe it started again, but, man, did it. Today after school I was halfway up the hill, walking home from the bus stop—Larry usually picks me up, but I figured he was over at the hospital again—when all of a sudden it was carrying on like you wouldn't believe, thunder and lightning and hail, even, and rain pouring down but good. And I guess there's just no place left for the water to go now, because in nothing flat there was this flood coming at me from gutter to gutter. I mean, the street wasn't a street anymore, it was like a regular river. And of course I got wet, but that wasn't so bad until the sidewalk ran out, and then it was all I could do to stay up on the curb. But even that wasn't too terrible until I came to this big bush that was right in the way. And while I was trying to get around it, my feet slipped out from under me, and then it was all over—I was smack on my backside in the middle of that muddy brown mess. Well, after that it was sort of like being on a giant lunatic's version of a water slide; I mean, I was shooting down the hill like some kind of Olympic bobsledder, and there wasn't a thing I could do but go along for the ride and try to steer clear of the cars I was whizzing past. Plus I lost my bookbag and one of my shoes and ripped my jeans and scraped my arms and legs all to pieces, and as for my rear end—well, you don't want to hear, trust me.

Larry was home after all when I finally limped through the front door. Turns out he had gone by the school for me when he saw it was going to rain, but I had already left on the bus. Sister came wagging her tail to meet me, and Larry hollered, "Is that you, Slim?" But he didn't even really look at me at first; the little half of a living room where we keep the dining room table was full of boxes and office furniture, and he had his head buried in this enormous crate with an overhead projector sticking out.

Right away I could feel my neck hairs getting prickly. It was all his commercial-art stuff, that's what it was, and I knew without asking that he'd quit his job and brought it all here so he could work at home and take care of Dad when he gets out of the hospital. I've heard them arguing about it over and over again: Dad doesn't want him to do it; he always says he's fine, just fine, and he doesn't need a nurse. And now Larry's gone and done it while he isn't here to stop him.

"Dad's not going to like this, Larry," I said. "You should have waited till he was home."

He turned around then, all full of apologies and explanations, but when he saw the mess I was in, his face changed.

"Oh, honey," he said, "what happened?"

"I slipped," I told him, and I went to shut myself in my bedroom. I just wasn't in the mood to have him getting all worried and worked up about me. I mean, if it was my dad it would be different.

But he didn't buy it. He followed me in and kept after me with his questions. All the time he was bringing washcloths and warm water and towels and that foul-smelling red medicine for my cuts, he just kept asking and asking in this quiet voice, "What happened, Slim?" and, "It's all right, you just tell me whenever you're ready," and, "How about I go heat up some of that tomato soup?" Until I couldn't hold it in any longer—I started blubbering out the whole story, and somehow the hill sliding got all mixed up with my dad being sick and that poor baby coming and that fool hello-saying myna bird. And next thing I knew, Larry was holding me in his lap like I was five years old or something and rocking me back and forth and patting me on the back and saying, "There, there," for crying out loud. I mean, that's only in the movies, isn't it? But here was big old Larry, rocking and patting and saying it anyway, "There, there, Slim honey, there, there."

Well anyhow, I finally calmed down a little. And then

we were both pretty embarrassed, just sitting there trying to act like everything was normal again, which is why I decided to come on to this meeting even though Larry wasn't going to make me and I really didn't feel much like it.

But I guess maybe the rain is getting to Ms. Crofford, too, because for the last twenty minutes she's been over there staring into space, and it's way past our notebook time, when finally she sort of comes to and notices the rest of us looking at her.

"I'm sorry," she says. "I was just thinking about a friend of mine who—about a friend of mine," she finishes lamely. And she tries to smile like usual, but this big fat bead of a tear goes rolling from her left eye down the side of her nose and ends up hanging there on the tip until there's nothing she can do but brush it off.

Oh Suzannah exchanges glances with Lorraine, and Roberto looks at Duke, and I can feel Isaiah's eyes on me. Oh, Lord, we're all thinking, what are we supposed to do when the *teacher's* got trouble?

And then before anybody can come up with an answer, a weird thing happens. This sweet little curly-haired lady, who's never raised that soft voice of hers above the level of those guys on the public radio, stands up with both her fists clenched and says loud enough for God to hear, "Oh, for heaven's sake, what am I *apologizing* for? My friend died today, my friend Tommy who was funny and smart and kind and a lot braver than I am, and I'm standing here *apologizing*? Well, I won't do it anymore, that's all. I'm mad and I'm not going to pretend I'm not. I come here every week pretending I know all the right things to say, but I don't. I don't know how to help any of you. I don't know how to make you tell me what's wrong. I don't know anything except that my friend is dead, and he shouldn't be, and talking isn't enough anymore. I'm mad and I want to *do* something. I want to *change* things."

The rain crashes down on the roof in the pause that follows, and it's as if the lightning has come inside. There's this electric current running around the room, and for the first time since the meetings began we're all wide awake. We're out of our chairs and we're surrounding Ms. Crofford, touching her arms and her shoulders and back and talking all at once:

Isaiah: "It's okay, Ms. Crofford. We're mad, too—"

Me: "We're all mad, Ms. Crofford—"

Roberto: "My brother shouldn't be sick either. This skinhead guy at school said he deserved it, and I punched him out, but that wasn't enough—"

Lorraine: "My mother can't stop throwing up—"

Duke: "My dad played football for USC, and now he looks like a skeleton—"

Suzannah: "My sister, she's all worried about that prom dress, and now the doctor says she might not even make it to Easter—"

"My brother—"

"My mother—"

"My sister—"

"My dad—"

"The baby, they don't know for sure—"

"So what do we do, Ms. Crofford? How can we change things?"

"If you'll tell us what to do—"

"Just tell us—"

"Then we'll *do* it, whatever it is—"

Ms. Crofford can't answer right away. She's nodding and squeezing our hands and smiling and crying all at once now, so Lorraine loans her a Kleenex from her purse-sized pack. And then Ms. Crofford blows her nose and takes a deep breath, and we wait for her to pull herself together a little, until finally she begins to speak again in a hiccupy, halting way:

"Thank you, Lorraine. Thanks, everybody. I didn't mean to—to make such a scene when you're just as—I mean, we're all in the same boat, aren't we? And there *are* things we can do, a thousand things like, well, like . . ."

"Like write the president!" shouts Isaiah, stepping in with his big eyes blazing. "And tell him we got to have more money for the scientists, however much it takes to find a cure, right?"

Oh, come on, Isaiah, get real.

But Ms. Crofford is nodding like this makes perfect sense. "Right," she says. "That's exactly right, Isaiah. Who's going to tell him if we don't?" Her voice cracks a little on the "if we don't," and she has to stop and blow her nose again before she can go on. "And there are plenty of others, too—senators and representatives, everybody who's supposed to be working for us—we could write every one of them, couldn't we? Every last one! And then we could—well, why don't you tell me, all of you—what else could we do? How can we help?"

We're all quiet for a moment, just standing here clueless. And then Suzannah looks sideways at Roberto. "Maybe we could help with the hot lines," she says. "There's this one guy my sister talks to all the time. She says he's better than medicine."

Well, it's a start anyway. I mean, Ms. Crofford says,

Great, terrific idea, and all that, but anybody can see it's Roberto that Suzannah's watching. He knows it, too, even though he's not about to look at her; he's too busy studying his left thumbnail. But he hears her all right. "My brother works the phones, when he's feeling okay," he says in a low voice. "Maybe she's been talking to him."

"Maybe so," says Suzannah, and I'm proud of her for not fainting on the spot. You can see the corners of her mouth going all dimply, where she's trying not to smile overmuch.

Lorraine, on the other hand, looks worried to death— like she's just been called on to list all the port cities of Argentina. "Sometimes—" she begins, and there are maybe a half dozen furrows between her eyebrows, "sometimes my mother stuffs envelopes. But I don't know with what, exactly," she adds apologetically. "And sometimes—" She hesitates again, and when she speaks, her voice is so small that we have to lean in to hear: "Sometimes she baby-sits cats."

Cats? Everybody just stares. But then Ms. Crofford— who is starting to seem like herself again—says, "Why, that's wonderful, Lorraine. That's important work. It's easy to forget how pets can suffer when their owners are sick."

Lorraine sighs and smiles a trembly smile; she's passed the pop quiz.

But now Ms. Crofford is saying, "Any more ideas?" and looking over here in my direction.

So I look at Duke.

And then everybody looks at Duke, and he turns bright red; I mean, even the tips of his ears are glowing, but he keeps those shoulders square. And it takes him a while, but finally he says, "My dad—he visits schools sometimes. To tell kids how to keep from getting sick." He pauses a moment, and then he lifts his chin, and somehow I know just how his father must have looked in a football helmet, ready to tackle the world. "It can happen to anybody, if they don't know."

Ms. Crofford nods; her gray eyes are all shiny. For a second I'm afraid she might try to hug old Harold, but fortunately she has better sense. "Your dad is saving lives," she says instead. "You must be very proud of him, Duke."

"Yes, ma'am," he says quietly.

I'm glad she remembered to call him by the right name.

But now she's back to me. "What about you, Slim—any thoughts?"

Oh, Lord. My mind's a blank. Everybody has already said everything there is to say, haven't they? I mean, writing letters and manning phone lines and visiting schools and feeding cats—those things are all we *can* do, aren't they? Even if they're not enough, not anywhere near enough . . .

I can feel Isaiah's eyes on me again, willing me to say something smart. Half-smart, even.

But all I can do is shake my head. "I don't know," I mutter. "I don't know anything."

Ms. Crofford pats my arm. "It's okay, sweetheart, take your time. We're all just searching here."

Take my time? With that damn cat clock ticking in my daddy's kitchen?

So I shake my head once more. I mean, where does that leave me but flat on my backside and halfway up the hill, sliding down and down and down?

Anyhow Ms. Crofford doesn't press; she's all excited about those letters, and she wants to know if we'd like to get going on them right now, this very minute. And the others say sure and start jotting down rough drafts in their notebooks: *Dear Mr. President, My name is Lorraine or Roberto or Duke, and my mother/brother/father has AIDS. . . .*

I can only guess what Isaiah is putting in his letter. He's over there writing furiously again, like he's out to do battle with that ballpoint.

And me, I'm just sitting here on my rear end, which to tell you the truth, is aching.

9 ✳

I MISS the next group meeting because my dad is coming home that afternoon, and I want to be there for that. They never did let me visit him in the hospital even though I got to talk to him on the phone almost every day and he kept telling me he was just fine. Still, I want to see with my own eyes.

He brings the sun with him. I guess that weird underwater baby out in the Pacific has finally stopped wailing, because they're saying on the weather reports that maybe we're done with the worst of the storms. The Hollywood sign is cloud-free for a change, bright white under shining blue skies, and even our mountains are back; the special-effects people have just finished hauling them in again when the red Toyota pulls into the driveway.

"Hello, girls!" Dad sings out first thing as Sister and I come running through the mess of fallen leaves and drying mud. "How many movie contracts did you two beauties turn down while I was gone?"

"Three for me and a miniseries for Sister," I answer,

trying to hold in my gladness at seeing him and trying *not* to see how thin he looks, all at the same time.

"Not bad for a slow month," he says, grinning and scratching Sister behind the ears. She's about out of her mind with joy, trying to leap through the open window to lick his face. And then, as Larry and I help him out of the car, he spies the banner I've tacked up over the front porch:

WELCOME HOME, DAD!!

"Thanks, sweetheart," he says quietly, putting his arm around me. It hardly weighs more than a hummingbird's wing, but oh, it feels good. And then I guess maybe he can feel me worrying all the way through my pores or something, so he clears his throat and goes into his Bob Hope voice: "And I want to tell you, folks, it's great to be back at the Palace. Here's one for you, Sister. Did you hear what the bartender said to the horse? 'So why the long face?' Ba-da-da-boom!"

That's his version of a rim shot, you see, which is what the drummer is supposed to make after every joke.

But when we get inside, Larry's new dining room decorations take him by surprise.

"What's all this?" he asks.

Larry tries to act like it's nothing. "Oh, you know, we talked a while back about my working here for a change, remember? I've been getting fed up with the commute anyhow and with having to answer to Ray Wilson over every little decision—"

"You quit?"

"Not *quit*, exactly. I'll be working at home, that's all. It's what I've been wanting to do for years."

Dad just looks at him, not fooled for a minute. And I know he's thinking what he's told Larry all along, and what I tried to tell him last week—that he's fine, just fine, and he doesn't want anybody making sacrifices for him. But now it's too late for arguments, isn't it? Which only makes it worse. I can see Dad struggling with what he wants to say, and Larry fiddling with some arrangement of pencils in a glass jar, hoping he won't say it.

Until finally Dad walks over and gives him a hug. "All right then, Mother Teresa," he says gently. "If it'll make you happy."

And Larry smiles at that, but he doesn't answer right away; he seems to be having some kind of trouble with his voice. "It'll make me happy," he manages at last.

For a moment the two of them just stand there quietly. And then Larry mumbles something about lasagna and hustles off to see about supper.

Dad watches him go. And after a second he clears his throat and turns around and winks at me. "Vat can I say, Doctor? Ze poor man is cuckoo!" He raises his eyebrows, twirls an imaginary mustache, and adds in his best stage whisper, "Ve must humor heem, you see."

Lord, it's good to have him home.

He hasn't been back half an hour and already the house seems like a different place—like it's come to life again—with the late-afternoon sun streaming in the windows and that Dixieland music he loves playing on the stereo and Sister bounding around after this crazy Super Ball that he's somehow managed to find for her at the hospital gift shop.

She's threatening to break every stick of furniture in the place, and normally Larry wouldn't approve, but now Dad's got him laughing too hard to even notice. I mean, I can't explain it: nearly all of his beautiful blond hair is gone, and there are these terrible blotches on his handsome face, and he's so skinny you can practically see through him, and yet here he is sitting at the kitchen table and just about killing Larry and me both with this insane imitation of his new buddy Jimbo—a three-hundred-pound night orderly who was always talking about his troubles with a wife he called Old Woolly.

" 'I'll tell you, Mack, Old Woolly has got me running so ragged this week, I don't know whether I'm going to be up to my bingo Thursday. The other night she fed me some of them french fried whaddayacallems, kazoonies or some such, and I'll swear I was up all night with the stomach-ache. . . . ' "

"Kazoonies?" Larry gasps. "What in the world are kazoonies?"

"That's just what I asked Jimbo," says Dad. "I said, 'Jimbo, do you maybe mean french fried zucchini?' And he said, 'Could be, Mack, could be. Zucchinis, kazoonies— same difference. They don't set too well is all I know.' "

We're practically on the floor when the doorbell starts ringing.

Rats, I'm thinking, running to answer it, *couldn't they wait even one night?* Dad has about a million friends is the thing, and he's crazy about every one of them. Which is why Larry has taken the phone off the hook and hasn't told a soul that Dad's coming home today. He thought it would be better if we could keep things quiet for the first twenty-four hours anyway.

But when I open the door, it's Isaiah and his mother who are standing on the front porch, holding grocery bags and looking worried.

Until they see me, that is, and their faces light up.

"Well, *here* you are, Slim!" says Mrs. Dodd. "And you look just fine, don't you, honey? You see, Isaiah, I told you she'd be fine!"

Isaiah just grins. "Hey, Slim, how you doin'?"

His mother gives me a hug and explains, "When you weren't at the group and we couldn't get through on the phone, we thought maybe something was wrong."

"No, ma'am, everything's fine," I say, trying to kind of ease the door closed in back of me before Dad sees them. Larry's right; it's too soon for him to be bothering with company. Then I add half in a whisper, "My dad just got home from the hospital."

"Oh, well, that's wonderful news!" Mrs. Dodd beams, and she starts handing me the bags. "We'll run right along then. We don't want to disturb him so soon, but maybe these will come in handy? Just a banana cake and a chicken casserole. We were thinking maybe you and Mr. Casey weren't feeling up to cooking."

"Slim? Who's there, honey?"

Oh, Lord, there's Dad and that's the end of it. We'll never get rid of them now. . . .

Still I give it my best shot: "It's Isaiah Dodd and his mother, Dad. They just dropped off some groceries, but they have to leave right away."

Too late. Here's Dad at the door already, shaking hands and brimming over with welcome, and Larry right behind him, looking only halfway alarmed. "What, Mrs. Dodd and her boy?" says Dad. "You mean the prophet Isaiah and angel Angelina, who took such good care of my best girl while I was gone?"

Naturally he doesn't say, "While I was sick," or, "While I was in the hospital." We're already pretending the last two weeks never really happened.

"Oh, it was nothing, just our pleasure, Mr. Mack," says the lady. "And now that goes double, seeing you home and looking so well."

Which is a flat-out lie if I ever heard one.

But Dad is laughing and shaking his shiny bald head. "Oh, no, ma'am, not me. I just washed both my hairs, and now I can't do a thing with them. But *you*—you're the one who looks marvelous! When's that little girl due, this spring?"

"The end of May," says Angelina, and she smiles and pats her belly like there's not a thing to worry about— which brings a funny kind of fluttering to my own stomach, for some reason. It's like that crazy little kick that my fingers refuse to forget; I mean, you'd almost think I'd swallowed it somehow.

Well, anyway, Dad won't hear of them leaving now. Angelina tries to protest, and Larry and I are still fretting about his overdoing, but he's more than a match for all of us once he sets his mind on hospitality. He's what you might call an irresistible force.

And, to tell you the truth, the evening doesn't turn out badly at all. The next thing I know, the five—or five and a half?—of us are sitting at the kitchen table (since the dining room is pretty much out of the question now), with Larry's lasagna *and* Angelina's casserole in front of us and that happy music playing, and Dad's slipping chicken to Sister under the table and telling us Jimbo's story about the time he got so mad at Old Woolly that he stormed out of the house without his pants on. And we're all just falling out laughing and having a wonderful time—almost like regular people, you know? Without a care in the world.

"Your dad's great," Isaiah says to me when the grown-ups have gone into the TV room to check out the tube situation and the two of us are clearing the table. "He makes everything funny."

"I know," I say, frowning a little as I scrape Dad's mostly untouched plate into the garbage sack. Shoot, I'm thinking, no mucho wonder he's so thin if he can't do any better than that. . . .

We're both quiet for a couple of minutes then, busy scraping and rinsing and loading up the dishwasher.

The sound of applause on "Wheel of Fortune" drifts over from across the hall.

"I'll spin," some contestant is saying.

"Oh, no, honey," Dad tells her, "life's too short. Solve the puzzle!" And then they're all laughing again.

Isaiah gives me one of his looks.

I keep scraping.

"We mailed the letters today," he says. "The first ones, I mean."

"Oh," I say. "Well, that's good."

"And Roberto says his brother can take us down to the hot-line office sometime, if we want to go. They might even let some of us start training—to talk to kids, you know?"

I can't help smiling. "You'd be good at that."

"I know," he says, smiling back. "Maybe we could go together sometime."

I shake my head. "I wouldn't know what to say."

"But they'd teach you, see? Then you'd know."

"Yeah, well . . . Maybe I'll just hang out with Lorraine and feed cats."

Isaiah chuckles. "She brought one today—mangiest-looking animal you ever saw. She said its name is Madonna."

"Hey, Slim! Isaiah!" It's Dad in the doorway, grinning. "Wanna watch *Boz*?"

My mom used to say he's like a small-town railroad station: no terminal facilities.

"Boz?" says Isaiah, looking interested.

But Angelina is right behind Dad, shaking her head. "No, thank you, Mack. We've had a wonderful time, but we really ought to be going. . . ."

"Oh, no, it's still early," says Dad, even though he's starting to look pretty ragged. He'd never admit it in a million years, but we can all see how tired he is. Angelina has sense enough not to mention it, though; she just keeps shaking her head and smiling and talking about how it's a school night, and Isaiah and I need our rest.

And then finally they're gone, and it's the best part of the evening, the part I've been waiting for: all of us together on the old green couch—me and my dad, with Sister at his knee, and Larry over on the other side—with our eyes on that yellow brick road.

"Hold you, honey," Dad whispers to me when the Flying Monkeys appear.

And at least for tonight—

With his arms tight around me—

We sneak past those suckers one more time.

10 ✳

My dad has started crocheting a blanket for Angelina's baby. He doesn't know the first thing about it, but he says Jimbo told him it was good for the nerves and he should know, otherwise Old Woolly would have put him in his grave by now. So Larry bought Dad a book that shows you how, plus those hooks and a bunch of yarn, and now it's pretty funny seeing him all tucked up on the couch, worrying over his chain stitch. Just call him Grandma Moses, he says.

He couldn't decide on the color at first. He said he knew the baby was a girl but he just couldn't face all that pink. But blue didn't seem right and Larry said, Well then why not yellow, you always liked that, and Dad said, Well yes, but he was also partial to green and gold and purple and red and even chartreuse and burnt umber. So then Larry got kind of impatient and said, Good grief, Mack, what do you want, the whole rainbow? That was when my dad's eyes lit up. Exactly, he said, that's exactly what I want—Larry Casey, you're a genius.

So anyhow now that's what he's doing—he's making the baby a blanket out of all the colors of the rainbow. And some people would maybe say it's too much or even sort of tacky, I mean no way would you ever see something like this in a department store. But Dad says that's the whole point—a gift that's one of a kind. And like Larry says, is it ever.

Ms. Crofford calls time, and I put down my pen, expecting the usual routine. It's been nearly half a month since I was here—I was out last week, too, because of a dumb cold. We're almost to the end of February now. Not that I really care; I figure one of these meetings is pretty much like another. But there's something new in the room today. Maybe it's just this nice weather we've had ever since the rain stopped, but you can feel it all around: Roberto is sitting up straight with both eyes open and even smiling a little and saying, "Cut that out!" when Suzannah tickles the back of his neck with the blue hair of this little plastic troll she's brought with her. And Lorraine is giggling and whispering into the ear of that poor old sorry-looking cat. And even Duke looks a little less out of place; he's still doodling those motorcycle skeletons all over his notebook, but somehow this week their grins seem almost cheery.

Anyway I just chalk up the good moods to barometric pressure until Ms. Crofford looks around at us with her eyes shining and says, "So has everybody heard the news?"

"What news?" I say, but the others are all nodding.

"About the carnival," Isaiah explains. "You remember, Slim, I told you on the phone. They're going to let us have a whole booth, right, Ms. Crofford?"

"Carnival?" I repeat, trying to think back to that conversation. My head was so stuffy and full of cold medicine, I really wasn't paying much attention.

So now everybody starts telling me at once: a bunch of PWA support groups from all over town are getting together in a couple of weeks to put on this big carnival that's supposed to raise money for all the things we're worrying about—research and hospices and help for people who are having trouble paying their medical bills or their rent or even buying groceries—stuff they've got to have *today*, this very minute. That's the beauty of it, Ms. Crofford says, we can really *do* something here, we can make a difference right now. And the organizers have been putting it together for months already, but there's still a lot of work left. And so Ms. Crofford asked, and even though it's late, they said sure, we can have a booth.

We just have to decide what kind.

"A fortune-teller!" says Isaiah.

"Cookies and cakes?" asks Lorraine.

"T-shirts!" says Suzannah. "My sister could teach us how to tie-dye. . . ."

"Maybe a live band," Roberto suggests. "I know a few guys. . . ."

"Or maybe a shooting gallery?" asks Duke.

Ms. Crofford nods and smiles at all of it, but now she's looking at me. "What about you, Slim? What kind of booth do you think we should have?"

Oh, Lord. Doesn't she ever give up? For a second I'm stuck all over again. I'm just sitting here like a piece of cheese.

And then Isaiah comes to the rescue. "Tell her about your dad, Slim!"

I'm still blank. "What about him?"

"You know, how he's an actor and all. I bet he could get some of his movie-star friends to come. We could sell autographs, maybe—"

"Movie stars?" Suzannah gasps. "Which ones?"

"I don't know. Whoever he wants, I guess," I say,

shrugging. I don't mean to brag, but it's just so great, this look that's on her face.

Lorraine's eyes are wide. "Madonna?" she whispers, and she's hugging the poor cat so tight, I'm afraid she's going to choke it.

"Well, I don't know about *her*," I admit. I can't lie to the poor kid; the disappointment might kill her later. "But he knows a lot of people on TV."

"Wonderful!" says Ms. Crofford, patting me on the back. "That sounds like a wonderful plan, Slim!"

I guess she's just so thrilled I've opened my mouth at all, she doesn't even notice that the whole thing was Isaiah's idea.

✳

THE NEXT two weeks fly by, what with so much getting ready. Ms. Crofford can't bring herself to say no to anybody, so our booth is going to be what she calls a potpourri, which means it will have a little bit of every-thing—fortune-telling and cookies and T-shirts and Ro-berto's band and even balloon popping with darts, which is actually a toned-down version of Duke's shooting gallery. And my dad is getting a whole raft of his actor friends to show up. Madonna couldn't make it, but his buddy Dave is coming; he used to be on that sitcom about the talking dummy, remember? And also Bob and Marietta and Rick from the old dinner theater and Dylan, the joke writer, and a bunch of TV-commercial people: Becky, the pain-relief lady, and Clare, who sells tofu burgers, and no telling who else, probably even Charlie from that stupid pilot and Bill and Sue, the Hearty Appetite Soup couple, and maybe Ed, the frozen broccoli guy, too.

"It'll be a party!" my dad says, smiling his happiest smile. It's the morning of the big day now, and we're all rushing around trying to get dressed and eat breakfast and make sure that Dad takes his medicine, which is a pretty big deal by itself, what with all the tablets he's supposed to put under his tongue and syrups for his coughing and powders that have to be dissolved in his tea.

We're just about done when Larry leaves the kitchen. He comes back a couple of minutes later looking kind of embarrassed for some reason and holding a medium-size box in his hands.

On the lid it says "Hollywood Hair."

He clears his throat. "I was just thinking—what I mean is, I thought you might like to see if—oh, hell, Mack, I got you a wig."

"Why, Larry," says Dad, taking the box from him and lifting out what looks at first glance like the lifeless carcass of a small blond animal, "it's—it's beautiful."

I can't tell if he wants to laugh or cry.

"Do you really think so?" asks Larry, looking hopeful. "I mean, you don't have to wear it if you don't want to. You're fine without it, but I just thought—well, you know, for the party—the carnival, that is—"

"I love it," says Dad. "It's exactly what I've been wanting." He puts it right on. "How's that?"

Good Lord. It's only a shade or two off from the right color, at least, but that's about the only kind thing I can say for it. And even Larry seems to be having second thoughts.

"Well now, wait a minute, Mack, you have to get it on straight, that's all. No, now that's too low in front. Just a little more to the—okay, that's better, that's almost—well, maybe I should go get a comb."

He leaves the room then, and Dad turns to me with his blue eyes dancing. "Is it as awful as it feels?" he whispers.

"Worse," I whisper back, trying not to laugh.

He nods and checks out his reflection in the glass of the oven door. "Just as I suspected," he says, shaking his head. "Doris Day without the soft focus."

"You've got to tell him," I say. I'm about choking on my giggles now.

"Not in a million years," says Dad, and he somehow manages to straighten out his face by the time Larry comes back, though I don't know how he does it. I myself have to leave the room three times during the comb-out, to keep from absolute hee-hawing.

Anyhow we're finally all wigged out and ready and halfway through the door when the phone starts ringing.

"Just let the machine answer it," says Larry. "We're late already."

But my dad can never ignore the phone; he's always afraid of missing something.

"Hello? Leland? Well, I'm just fine, honey. How are you?"

It's my mother.

My heart gives the nervous little skip—half-glad, half-scared—that it always does when she calls, which she does at least twice a week. Glad because she's my mom and I miss her, scared because this might be the time that she'll try to make me go back.

Dad is winking at me as he talks into the phone. "Slim? You mean that gorgeous blond starlet who hangs around here sometimes? Oh, yes, she's fine. Better than fine. As a matter of fact, she's perfect. Would you like to speak to her?"

I take the phone from his outstretched hand. "Hi, Mom."

It's not that I'm worried about her thinking that I'm going to catch the virus from living with my dad; she knows better than that. It's just that she'd never want me to have to see him feeling bad, even—or to see *any* kind of sickness or suffering, if she could help it. Plus she might think I'd be in the way. And besides, she misses me, too. But I *can't* leave, I *won't* leave—

"Slim? How's everything, sweetheart?"

It's no big deal, after all. She just wants to know if I'm okay, and how did I do on that math test last Wednesday, and did we remember my appointment at the dentist? So I say everything's great and pretty good, *B* minus, and, Yes, ma'am, only one little cavity. And she says, Well, that's not bad at all—in that tone that really means *B plus* and *no* cavities would be better, but nice try anyway—and then she tells me all the news from Shreveport, Louisiana, which is where the microchips are selling now: what an awful time Alex is having with his left knee from that jogging accident last month; and how beautiful the azaleas are—she can't believe they're out already; and oh, by the way, wouldn't I like to come home for the Easter holidays?

But I am home, Mama, is what I'm thinking. Only what I say is I would but I can't—we've only got that Thursday and Friday off from school, and I'll probably have to be working on my science project the whole time.

"Oh, well," she says, and even from fifteen hundred miles away, I can hear her sighing. "Summer vacation will be here before we know it, right? I guess I can hold out till then."

Which makes me ache a little. I mean, it's just so hard, all this *choosing*.

Across the kitchen Dad is making clown faces and bending down to let Sister sniff his wig. Larry is already outside, warming up the Toyota.

"Listen, Mom, I'm sorry, but I've got to run. There's this carnival we're going to."

"A carnival?" My mother has never been a big fan of carnivals—too much noise and too many crowds—but now she sounds almost as if she wishes she were going with us. "Well, you have a good time, sweetheart. I love you. I'll talk to you soon—"

"Okay, Mom, I love you, too."

I hang up the phone and take a deep breath that I let out slowly. It feels like I've just run a mile.

Dad comes over and gives my shoulders a squeeze. "Everything all right?" he asks.

The wig has slipped sideways again.

"Just fine, Doris," I answer, grinning.

I'll cross that summer-vacation bridge when I come to it, I guess.

11 ✻

THE CARNIVAL is already in full swing down near Zuma Beach by the time we get there—the merry-go-round whirling away and kids shrieking on the Mad Mouse and the Ferris wheel and the Salt and Pepper Shaker, and that good old cheesy carnival music clashing with the heavy-metal howling that's booming out of Roberto's speakers. And everywhere there are smiling faces and voices calling and babies losing bright-colored helium balloons that go floating up into that blue, blue sky, where the L.A. sea gulls don't even give them a second glance. I guess nothing surprises those birds.

Meanwhile there's a whole ocean lying just beyond all this carrying on, sparkling its heart out.

"Oh, yes," says my dad, breathing in the day. "Now this is more like it!"

Even the Pacific Ocean looks pale up against his shining eyes.

"Mack's here!" somebody shouts.

"Hey, Mack!"

"How you been, buddy?"

"Great to see you, Mack!"

They're all around us before you can blink—not just the ones I expected, but Allison and Angie and Hilary, too, and Peggy and Willie and June and Mitch and Francie and Jackie and I don't know who all—hugging and laughing and clapping us on the back while they lead us over to the Potpourri Booth.

"Where you been, Mack? We've been waiting for you!"

"Sorry we're late, guys. We had to run by the cleaners and get my wig pressed."

"Hey, Slim! Over here!"

It's Isaiah hollering at me from inside the booth. They've got him selling tickets between the T-shirt display—where Suzannah and a pale dark-eyed girl in a wheelchair are doing a brisk business—and a star-spangled black curtain with the words MADAME ANGELINA TELLS ALL spelled out in glittery letters.

"How's it going?" I ask him as he lifts the hinged panel in the wooden counter to let me in.

"Great!" he shouts over the noise of the crowd and the screeching of the guitars and the sudden pops from Duke's balloon concession. He rattles his boxful of receipts. "We're cleaning up!"

"Is that Slim?" Mrs. Dodd's voice calls.

"Yes, ma'am," I answer.

She pushes aside the curtain and sticks out her red-turbaned head. "Come into my parlor, my dear," she says, smiling mysteriously. "The future holds no secrets for Madame Angelina!"

"Well, look at you, girl!" my dad calls to her, grinning from ear to ear. "Are you lonesome in there all by yourself?"

She grins back. "Oh, it's not so bad—kind of peaceful, really."

"Peaceful?" Dad sounds horrified. "Well, we can fix that! Right this way, folks—your questions answered, your love lives mended, the mysteries of the ages plumbed, and all for only two bucks and change!" And pretty soon his buddies are crowding in together, and he's introducing everybody to everybody:

"Well, hello, Lorraine—you are Lorraine, aren't you, honey? Did you make all these beautiful cookies yourself? And this pretty lady must be your mom! How are you, ma'am? I'm Mack and this is Gerry and Gary and Sidney and Jan and Yvonne and Pam and Annie and Roger and . . ."

It takes him maybe five minutes to be best friends with the entire booth and to have the whole gang laughing and talking all at once—not just little old Lorraine and her sweet-faced mother, but Ms. Crofford, too (Barbara honey, he calls her), and Duke and his big skinny dad and Roberto and his tough-looking brother and Suzannah's dark-eyed sister and Suzannah herself, who pretty near passes out when she meets the broccoli guy.

"You look just like you *look*!" she tells him, and he says, "Well, thanks," and before long she's got him and all the other TV people autographing T-shirts and posing for instant pictures and telling their life stories into a video camera.

"What about you, Mr. McGranahan?" she asks. "Do you have any advice for young people who want to get into show business?"

"Only this," says my dad, nodding wisely. "It does no good to remember lines if you can't remember who says them."

It's a wonderful day, all in all, the best I can remember in a long, long time. We laugh and sing and dance to Roberto's god-awful music and gorge on popcorn and hot dogs and gaze into Madame Angelina's crystal ball. And when every last cookie and T-shirt have been sold and the thousandth balloon has popped, we ride all the rides three times over.

"Let's try the Ferris wheel again," says my dad. "We'll get a great view of the sunset from up top."

Larry gives me a look, like *Can you believe this guy?* "I don't know, Mack. Maybe we ought to think about going home," he says. "Better hit the freeway before dark."

It's not really the freeway he's worrying about.

"But it's still early!" says Dad. He's worse than any kid at Christmas—too stubborn to know he's exhausted. "We don't want to miss the lights, do we, Slim? That's the best part!"

How does he do it? I ask myself. By now I'm so tired I can hardly see straight. "Whatever you guys want," I say, leaning up against the side of the booth. I guess it isn't really all that late, just that nowhere time, you know? Not day and not night, not one thing or the other. But my eyelids are drooping anyhow, and I'm seeing two of everything— two merry-go-rounds and two Mad Mice and twice the crowds and double the confusion—

And look over there—two big black trucks. What are trucks doing inside the carnival? I wonder. I must be half-asleep, dreaming or something, because all of a sudden these big clumsy four by fours come crashing through the temporary fences with the weirdest-looking drivers you ever saw—squinty-eyed bald guys leaning out the windows and hanging on to the sides and shaking baseball bats and fists in our faces—

"Perverts!" they're screaming. "Get out of our country! Take your sicko queer diseases and die somewhere else!"

Are those *swastikas* on their arms?

You *are* dreaming, I tell myself. Or somebody's making a movie—

That's when the first bottle smashes against the post beside me.

"Get down, Slim!" my dad and Larry say at the same time, and they both step in front of me with their arms spread wide. "Get down, everybody! Stay back!"

There are bottles shattering everywhere now, and girls screaming and babies crying and people running every which way.

"Get down! Stay down!" Dad and Larry keep shouting. They've got me pressed so hard into the wooden counter that I can scarcely breathe.

And then it's over as suddenly as it began. Policemen appear out of nowhere as the trucks crash through another part of the fence and go screeching off onto the highway, and sirens start to wail.

We're all still frozen, standing like statues. Even the merry-go-round has stopped whirling, though its sappy music plays on:

> *All around the mulberry bush*
> *The monkey chased the weasel. . . .*

My dad turns to me. "You all right, honey?" he asks anxiously, checking me up and down. "That glass didn't hurt you, did it?"

I shake my head. "I'm fine."

He hugs me and looks around. "It's okay, everybody. It's over. Is everybody okay?"

For a wonder, nobody is hurt. Just scared and shaken, pale as ghosts—

And Lorraine has the hiccups again. "Are they g-gone?" she whispers, peering out from her mother's arms.

My dad touches her hair. "They're gone, sweetheart," he says. "Don't be afraid." There's something in his face I've never seen before. A muscle twitches in his jaw, like he's gritting his teeth. And then before I can give it a name, the look has vanished, and he's back to his clowning: "Hey, Lorraine," he says real quietlike, as if he's telling her some big secret, "I bet I know what those skinheads wanted."

"Wh-what?"

He gives her a wink and walks a little way out of the booth, where he cups his hands around his mouth and calls out onto the highway: "Just follow the signs to Melrose Avenue, fellas! You can't miss it—it's a little place called Hollywood Hair!" And then he takes his wig right off his head and tips it like a hat.

That does the trick somehow. Lorraine smiles through her tears, and somebody starts to laugh. And pretty soon everybody is laughing. The lights come on, and the merry-go-round cranks up, and Dad and his actor buddies are firing off skinhead jokes:

"Did you see that big one? Talk about *ugly*!"

"He's so ugly, when he was born, the doctor slapped his mother!"

"He's so ugly, when you look up *ugly* in the dictionary, his picture's there!"

"And *dumb*? Listen—"

"He's so dumb, he thinks the Kentucky Derby is a hat!"

"He's so dumb, he picked up a pile of dog do and said, 'Look what I almost stepped in!'"

"He's so ugly..."

"He's so dumb..."

"He's so ugly *and* dumb..."

And I'm laughing right along with the rest; I'm laughing till it hurts, till the tears are streaming down my face and I ache all over. But at the same time I'm shaking my head; I don't understand at all. "How can we laugh?" I ask Angelina, wiping my eyes. "How can my dad make us laugh when it's all so awful?"

"Oh, honey," she says, putting her arm around me, "he has to make us laugh. That's his sword and shield, don't you see?"

His sword and shield?

I follow her look, and what I see is this: my dad in the middle of the laughing crowd, with his blue eyes dancing and some joke on his lips and that terrible wig sliding south. And those lights he didn't want to miss are glittering all around him, shutting out the dark, dark night.

12 ✳

I GUESS the excitement at the carnival was too much for my dad, or maybe it was something he ate—or *didn't* eat, more likely. Anyway the next day he's all done in: he's shivering one minute and sweating the next, and he can't stop throwing up. And Larry's all for taking him back to the hospital, but Dad doesn't want to go, and this time the doctor agrees with him for some reason. He says to watch him for a couple of days and see what happens.

So we watch and we wait and we try not to panic, and sure enough the worst is over by Thursday, though he's still weak as water. When I get home from school, he's tucked up on the old green couch again, working on the baby's blanket.

"Hello, gorgeous," he says. There are circles the color of bruises under his eyes, but he's smiling just like always. "How was your day?"

"Pretty good." I try to keep the worry out of my voice as I sit down beside him and give Sister's head a pat; she's lying at his feet as usual. "How was yours?"

"Perfect," he answers, holding up his masterpiece for my inspection. "What do you think?"

"It's—it's terrific, Dad. It's real—colorful."

He chuckles. "You're a terrible liar, little Slimderella. It's a mess, that's what it is. Don't worry, I know I've made a couple of mistakes, but I can fix 'em. I've got it all planned. I just have to rip out this piece of blue over here and move it by the yellow, don't you think? And then that'll take care of this other little goof with the reddish orange; I've got it way too close to the turquoise. And after that—well, I know it's kind of hard to picture right now, but it's gonna be great, I guarantee it."

"Sure, Dad," I say, even though he's already started over so many times that I can't help having my doubts. I mean, at this rate Angelina's baby will be out of college before it's done.

The phone starts ringing.

"I'll get it," I say quickly, to keep Dad off his feet. I expect it'll be one of his buddies again; they've been calling every five minutes, wanting to know if he's feeling any better.

But it's Isaiah, for me.

"You've got to come over here!" he's hollering. "Right now, do you hear me, Slim? Right this minute!"

Oh, Lord. His mom—or the baby? It's all I can do to make myself say, "What's wrong, Isaiah? What's the matter?"

"Nothing's the matter. Everything's *great!*" he shouts. I have to hold the phone at arm's length to keep my eardrum in one piece. "Man, you won't believe it!"

"Believe *what?*" I ask him. I can't decide if I'm more

relieved or put out, now that I know he's scared me for nothing. "You'll have to tell me, Isaiah—I can't come over. Larry just dropped me off. He's gone to the grocery store."

"Aw, man, but I wanted you to *see*, see? I'd bring it over there, but I don't have a ride either. My mom's at her Lamaze class. Well, shoot, I'll just have to wait and show you at the meeting tomorrow, I guess—"

"Isaiah Dodd, don't you do that to me. Don't you dare call over here and nearly give me a heart attack and then hang up without telling me what you're talking about!"

"Aw, shoot, Slim. I wanted to *show* you—"

"Isaiah!"

I can hear him sighing. "Oh, well, all right. It won't be the same, but you'll just have to try to see it in your head, okay?"

"See *what*, for pete's sake?"

"The letter," he says, and his voice goes all low and trembly. "The letter that was in the mailbox when I got home from school just now. The letter to me, Isaiah Dodd, Esquire, at the Royal Palm Apartments in West Hollywood, California, from the *president of the United States*!"

"You're kidding me."

"No, ma'am, I'm holding it right here in my hand."

"He *wrote you back*? The president actually wrote *you*?"

"That's what I said." I can feel Isaiah grinning all the way through the phone lines.

"No way—"

"I'm telling you, Slim—I've got it right here! Shoot, I knew you'd never believe it without seeing it. You're like old what's-his-name, doubting Thomas."

"I am not. It's just—well, the president must get a

million letters every day. How's he gonna answer all of 'em?'"

"Who says he answers *all* of 'em?"

"Oh, for crying out loud, Isaiah, what's it say anyhow?"

I can just see him sitting up all proud over there, holding the page close to his glasses. " 'Dear Mr. Isaiah Dodd,' " he reads, " 'Thank you for writing to express your concern about the AIDS crisis. I am truly sorry to hear of your family's trouble, and I want you to know that I strongly support all the tireless efforts that are being made every day by people like you in the battle against this great national calamity....' "

It goes on from there to list a whole heap of bills and resolutions and I don't know what all that the Congress has already passed, or is thinking about passing, or would really *like* to pass if it only had the money, and to tell how the president himself is personally doing everything he possibly can. I mean, the way he talks, you'd think we'd be bound to have this whole thing licked in a month or two, tops. And then he wraps it all up by saying:

" 'And in conclusion, Mr. Dodd, let me say again that I share your concern and that I appreciate your taking the time to voice your opinion. My family joins me in extending the warmest of wishes to you and your family, especially in these difficult times. Our prayers are with you, etc., etc. Sincerely, etc., etc.' "

"That's great, Isaiah," I say when he's finally done. "That's one heck of a letter, all right." But inside I'm thinking, Shoot, doesn't he know it's just a *form* letter? Some clerk in the mail room punched it out on a computer and filled in the right names, that's all....

Meanwhile Isaiah sounds like he's practically flying around over there.

"I know, I just can't believe it! I mean, I thought maybe I'd get a postcard or something, but *this*—oh, man, wait'll Mama sees it!"

"What's wrong, honey?" my dad asks as soon as I hang up the phone.

"Nothing," I start to say, but it's no use; he can see right through me. So I go sit beside him again and tell the whole story, and he says not to worry, that I did the right thing, not bursting Isaiah's bubble. "Who knows," he says, "maybe his letter to Washington was so wonderful that the president really did answer it personally."

"Oh, Dad—"

"O ye of little faith," he teases, ruffling my hair. "When did you stop believing in Santa Claus, little girl?"

"When you fell off the roof with all those sleigh bells," I remind him, "and poor Sister was stuck up there with cardboard antlers on her head."

"*Oh*, yes," he groans, leaning over to give Sister an apologetic pat. "Sorry about that, ladies."

"It's okay. We didn't mind, did we, Sister? At least I didn't. I think I liked it better, knowing it was you."

"Really?" Dad looks like he finds this hard to believe.

But I'm nodding. "You remember those pictures you bought at the mall every year, with me in Santa's lap, screaming my head off? I mean, who *was* that fat guy anyhow?"

"Such a sensible child," he says, chuckling. "My daddy was convinced you'd end up on the Supreme Court. Judge Roy Mae Bean—that's what he called you."

Neither of us says anything for a minute; we're just

sitting there peacefully with the sound of Sister's dog breath in our ears and Dad's crochet hook whispering through the wool. And then—

"Slim . . ."

"Yessir?"

"Listen, honey, I talked to your mother today—"

"Mom called?" Right away I'm suspicious. "Didn't she know I'd be at school?"

"Well, yes, but she was going to be at a meeting later. She just wanted to remind you that your grandmother's birthday is coming up next week, that's all. She thought you might want to send a card."

"Oh," I say, breathing again. "Sure."

"She sent her love, too."

Quiet again: *shh, shh, shh . . .*

"Slim?"

"Yessir?"

"If you ever—well, I've been doing some thinking the last couple of days, you know?"

While he was sick, he means.

"And anyhow today after your mom called, Larry and I got to talking and—"

"Talking about what?" I interrupt. There go those neck hairs again.

He doesn't answer right away; he's choosing his words one by one, I guess. And finally he says, "Look, sweetheart, you know how I love having you here with me, don't you?"

"Y-yessir—" There are caution lights blinking all over my brain: *Watch what you say, girl; this could be a trap. . . .*

"But your mom—well, she misses you, kiddo. Just like I would."

I'm already shaking my head. "I'm not leaving," I say. "I want to stay here with you."

"Oh, Slim—I want you here, too. You know that. But what I'm trying to say is, if you ever think you'd like to go back there with her—just for a while, not forever—well, it would be okay, that's all. You wouldn't be deserting me or anything like that."

"I'm not leaving. Don't make me leave, Dad—"

I can't say any more; my throat is all clodded up again.

Dad doesn't talk either for a couple of minutes. He's dropped the crochet hook and is holding my hand like that other time, like he'd drown without it.

Somehow Sister knows that something is wrong. She stands up and looks at us and whines a little, then pushes her nose at my dad's sleeve until he has to smile and scratch her behind the ears.

"Oh, stop, Sister," he tells her. "This isn't the death scene from *Camille*. You don't even speak French, remember?"

Which makes *me* smile, too, just like he wants.

A couple minutes more tick by on the cat clock. And then Dad says quietly:

"It might get kind of rough, honey. Later on, I mean."

"I don't care."

"Okay. But there's no law against changing your mind, right, Your Honor?"

I don't answer. Fat chance, is what I'm thinking.

13 ✳

BUT I THOUGHT there'd be more time.

I could look on the calendar and find the exact date when the monkeys start flying again. It's March fifteenth. I know because I marked a big *X* on it to remind me to send my grandmother that card and also because my dad points to it the next morning at breakfast and then says it as a joke:

"Beware the ides of March."

"What's that?" I ask with my mouth full of Frosted Mini-Wheats.

"*Julius Caesar*, act one, scene two," he says, grinning. "My first play ever. I was Caesar in Mr. Chuck Krohn's sophomore English class production at Mirabeau B. Lamar High School, and my friend Leroy Cataline was the Soothsayer."

"What's a soothsayer?"

"A Roman psychic—you know, the guy who has to warn Caesar that they'll be out to get him on the fifteenth: 'Beware the ides of March!'" Dad chuckles. "Poor old Leroy, he was so nervous, he practiced that line every way you could possibly say it: 'Be*ware* the ides of March' and 'Beware the *ides* of March' and '*Be*ware *the* ides *of* March'— until his brains were so scrambled, it didn't make a bit of sense to him anymore. And finally it's the day of our one and only performance with the whole school sitting out there staring at him, and you know what he says?"

I shake my head.

" '*Be*ware *the wides of arch!*' "

"Oh, no!" I sputter, choking on my Mini-Wheats.

"Oh, yes. Sounded like a shoe salesman telling Caesar he'd better go for a double *D* in that next pair of sandals. I swear, it's a wonder Mr. Krohn didn't kill us both, the way we were rolling around out there. . . ."

That's the last I remember laughing in March.

The throwing up starts again right after breakfast, even though he hasn't eaten anything but a couple of bites of oatmeal.

"Maybe I should stay home today," I tell Larry, but he says that's silly, it would just upset my dad if I missed school because of him. And I know he's right so I go, even though I don't hear a word the teacher says all day. The only thing I know is she's up there reading that depressing poem about the talking blackbird that I already heard last year—you know, "Quoth the raven" and all that—when the last bell finally rings.

I'm the first one outside, waiting for Larry's red Toyota to turn in the driveway.

"Isn't that your dad's car in front of the office?" Anne Smiley asks as her mother's station wagon pulls up. She's pointing to somebody else's little red something or other.

"No," I tell her. "And he's not my dad—" I try to

explain about Larry, but she's not listening; she's gone already.

I kick at a rock. "He's not my dad," I mumble again under my breath.

When I first registered for school out here, we had a whole pile of forms to fill out, and in the place where you have to put who you live with and their relationships to you and all that, I got stuck.

"What do I put down for Larry?" I asked. "I mean, he's not my dad or mom or aunt or cousin or stepfather or—"

"Just put down *friend*," my dad told me, so that's what I did. But I don't know, it never seemed exactly right.

Anyway Larry is usually the first one here, but today he doesn't come and doesn't come, and I'm about to give up and go get in the bus line when a sky blue Volkswagen bug comes putt-putting up to the curb.

"Hey, Slim!" Isaiah hollers, leaning out the window. "Come on, you're riding with us today!"

"What's wrong?" I ask with my heart in my mouth, climbing in behind Angelina. "It's my dad, isn't it?"

"He's all right, sweetheart. Larry just wanted the doctor to have a look at him, that's all. And since we were coming by here on the way to the group anyhow, it was easy for us to stop."

The group—I had forgotten. Shoot, I'm really not in the mood today.

But Isaiah's about ten feet off the ground, even squinched up there in that little front seat. He's hanging on to that letter of his like it's pure gold.

"I can't wait to show everybody," he says after I've looked at it and done the best I can with "Wow" and "Great" and all. "They're not gonna believe it!"

Which just makes my stomach hurt, you know? Beware the ides of March or the wides of arch or whatever the heck they are. . . .

Sure enough, when we get there Suzannah and Duke and Roberto and Lorraine are all waving around their envelopes from Washington, too, and when they start comparing letters, it's just what I was afraid of—they're all exactly alike except for the names. And naturally Ms. Crofford tries to say it doesn't matter; they're still wonderful:

"Of course the president can't answer every bit of his mail personally. Who'd run the country if he did? But these are still official White House correspondence, don't you see?"

Maybe. But everybody's pretty let down anyway. I mean, face it, a computer letter from some secretary just ain't what they had in mind.

Isaiah's shoulders are sagging. Shoot, I'm thinking, I guess I should have told him, after all. So much for the fat man in the red suit, Dad. . . .

But Ms. Crofford is just getting started.

"Oh, come on, guys—we should be celebrating! The carnival was a huge success. I'm so proud of all of you! Did you know that our booth was one of the biggest money raisers of the whole day? We made a difference, a real difference, don't you see? We put food on people's tables and medicine, too, and now these letters—well, maybe I should have explained before, but I never expected any kind of reply at all, to tell you the truth. Because that's not what matters. What matters is that you stood up to be counted. You made your voices heard, don't you see? And the more voices they hear in Washington, the more likely they are to start *listening*!"

Isaiah is standing up a little straighter now. "So what you're saying is we ought to write another one?"

"Exactly!" says Ms. Crofford. "The sooner, the better! And if another form letter comes, then we'll wear it as a badge of honor. We'll collect a stack of them as high as a mountain, and the day the scientists announce that they've found a cure, we'll light the biggest victory bonfire there ever was!"

But will my dad be around for the party? I wonder.

Isaiah is already over there nodding and pulling out his notebook, which just makes me ache more somehow. But nobody else seems all that charged up by the rah-rah speech.

"Yeah, well, I guess that's something anyway," says Suzannah. I should have known she'd be another one who'd pretty much flip out over this whole letter-from-the-president-himself deal, him being a celebrity and all. I mean, the kid looks like she's about to cry.

Which really gets to me for some reason, not being in the greatest of moods myself. "Something," I repeat under my breath. "Something ain't worth squat."

"Yeah, well, it beats the heck out of *nothing*," says Suzannah, looking right at me. "Which is all some people around here have done."

I feel the blood rushing to my face. "Are you talking to me?" I ask, gritting my teeth.

"What do you think?" she shoots back.

I'm seriously considering punching her in the nose when Ms. Crofford steps in between us. "Now, girls, there's no reason to get upset. We're all just tired," she's saying in her most soothing voice, while Isaiah appears as if by magic at my left elbow: "Forget it, Slim, she don't mean anything."

I just stand there for a minute, glaring at everybody and

blinking back the stupid tears that are trying to crowd their way into my eyes. No way *I'm* going to cry, for pete's sake. "Aw, to heck with all of y'all," I mutter finally. "I'm outa here."

Which would have been a great exit line if only I had a horse tied up outside so I could go galloping off into the sunset. Or a limo, maybe, or shoot, even a pair of roller skates—I'm not proud. But unfortunately there's nothing, and it's a good six miles from here to my house, and that's with a couple of freeways and four or five fair-size hills in between.

And besides, Barbara honey is pretty quick on her feet, gray hairs and all. I'm hardly out the door before she's coming after me and trying to smooth everything over. And she looks so upset herself that I'm afraid *she'll* go on another crying jag if I don't go back in.

So I do.

But that bad feeling that's been in my stomach all day keeps getting stronger and stronger, and I don't know what anybody says the rest of the meeting. I'm just sitting here thinking about my dad and breaking all his rules, trying to worry him well. And when our time is finally up, and Isaiah and I go out to his mom's car, I don't say a word while Angelina tells me gently that the doctor has decided to put my dad back in the hospital, after all. It feels as if I've known it for months.

I wonder if old Caesar knew what was coming, too.

14 ✳

THIS TIME my dad is in the hospital three weeks, not two, and when he comes home, he looks worse than he did when he went in.

"Hello, girls," he says to me and Sister as we run out to meet him again. He's smiling just like the last time.

Only it's not like the last time at all. Today he's so weak, he can barely get out of the car, and Larry and I have to practically carry him into the house between us. Not that there's much to carry; I thought he was thin three weeks ago, but that was nothing compared to now. He's just bones is all, with that poor splotched skin holding them together, and a skull with blue eyes looking out of it. Or trying to, at least; one of his eyes is halfway closed by a Kaposi's sarcoma lesion that's got the lid all swollen up and sore looking.

"It's good to be home," he says.

He's too tired to talk much, but he sits up on the couch with us for a little while, with his arm around me, smiling and listening to me tell all the news. All that I can think of anyhow. It isn't much really, but I feel like somebody ought to be saying *something:* school is the same as always, I have to do a paper on General Cornwallis for history, I got a *B* on that science project—which I ended up throwing together at the last second on Easter night—

"Tell him what you did," says Larry, trying to help.

"Oh, it was nothing," I say with a shrug. " 'Earthshine,' I called it. That's sunlight reflected from the earth to the moon—it's why you can sort of make out the dark part, you know? You get a flashlight, see, that's supposed to be the sun, and you shine it right straight at a blue ball that's supposed to be the earth. And then you get a little white ball for the moon—the new moon, I mean, the one that's all dark, remember? And you put 'em all on coat hangers in a big black box with a peephole, and—well, the earthshine doesn't really shed all *that* much light, at least mine didn't. Maybe that's why I only got a *B*. But that's the idea anyway."

"Pure genius," says my dad, tapping my brow. "I didn't understand a word so it must be marvelous. And what about the group—everything okay there?"

I shrug again. "I guess." But Larry gives me a look, so I can't just let it drop. "Well, I don't know, exactly. I didn't feel like going the last couple of times."

"Oh." I can see my dad thinking this over, then deciding not to push it. "But Isaiah's all right—and his mama?"

"Oh, sure, except—well, Angelina's starting to get kind of tired, but the doctor says that's normal. It's only six weeks now till the baby's due." I don't see any point in mentioning just *how* tired she looked the last time I was over there. It scared me a little, to tell the truth. But Dad doesn't need all that on his mind right now.

"Six weeks?" He's shaking his head. "I'd better get busy

on that blanket!" He looks at Larry. "Time's a-wastin',
right, Old Woolly?"

Larry smiles. "Right, Jimbo," he says, and then he clears
his throat and gets up like he's in a big hurry all of a sudden.
"Better go see if that oven is preheated yet. . . ."

✳

BUT A WEEK later the blanket is no further along than
it was a month ago. Dad's sleeping so much is why; it's like
he's just bone tired all the time. And when he's awake, the
least little thing wears him out.

I find him with the blanket in his lap and his eyes half-
closed when I come home from school the next Wednesday.

"Why don't you stretch out for a while, Dad?" I say. "I
could run get you a pillow—"

"Hmm? Oh, hello, honey. Was I nodding? Well, shoot,
I meant to get at least two more rows done today." He grins
and lifts the hook up and down like a miniature weight.
"Gonna have to start working on my triceps. Can't even
handle this little old fifty-pounder anymore."

Even the crochet hook is heavy now?

"Could you show me how it works?" I ask quickly, to
cover the ache this brings. "I've been wanting to learn."

"Really?" He looks at me for a second, seeing everything I'm thinking. And then he smiles. "Well, sure, baby,
it's easy. You just make a little loop like so, and then you
catch it right here and pull it back, you see? You try it now.
That's right, that's the idea—"

"Oh, no, look—I've messed it all up!"

"Oh, that's nothing. We can fix that. You just rip it out
and start again, that's all. We'll have it right in no time."

Ten minutes later he's asleep again.

It's no wonder, though; I mean, how's he going to get his strength back if he never eats? He's like a little kid that way; half the time he sneaks his food to Sister, until Larry says she has to stay outside during dinner, and once we catch him wrapping up his turkey in his napkin.

"Oh, Mack," says Larry, but Dad just winks at me and says he was going to save it for later.

But I won't smile like he wants me to because there's nothing funny about it. He's always saying how good everything looks and smells and what a good cook Larry is, and then he takes maybe two bites. "Delicious," he swears, and at the same time he's just pushing the food around his plate, hiding the peas under a lettuce leaf or whatever.

Meanwhile he doesn't even weigh half as much as I do, I bet, and I'm a foot shorter and the skinniest kid in my class.

"He can't go on like this," I tell Larry privately, while Dad's sitting at the living room window, half-dozing, watching the hummingbirds at the feeder Larry's fixed up outside. "Maybe—well, maybe we ought to ask the doctor. Maybe he ought to go back to the hospital—they can give him that food in the tubes there, can't they? Like they did before? Maybe he came home too soon this time. Maybe his stomach just wasn't ready yet."

Larry shakes his head. "Slim—" he begins, and then he stops.

"What?" I ask him. "That makes sense, doesn't it? I mean, sure, I know he hates the hospital, but he's got to have food, Larry. He's getting like those people with that what-do-you-call-it, anorexia—they showed us a film about it at school. That can *kill* you, you know?"

But Larry won't look at me. He's stirring up this special yogurt and banana mixture to make into bread or muffins or some such, even though there's no way Dad's ever going to eat more than a mouthful. "We've already talked to the doctor, Slim."

"You have? Well, what did he say? Does he think Dad ought to have those tubes again or—"

"No, honey, he thinks—well, I really shouldn't be saying, Slim; it's your dad who ought to talk to you about all this—"

"About all what? About him not wanting to go back to the hospital? Shoot, Larry, I told you, I know he doesn't want to, but we just have to *make* him if the doctor says he should!"

"Slim—" Larry puts down the spoon finally and looks at me. "The doctor doesn't say that, sweetheart. He thinks this last time at the hospital—well, it didn't help, that's all. And now he says if your dad wants to be at home, then maybe that's what's best for him."

I just stand there for a minute, staring at him, trying to understand what he's said.

Tick, tick, tick, tick, tick, tick, tick . . .

"You mean—" I begin, but my voice isn't working right, and I have to try again. "You mean he's given up, don't you? You mean the doctor's given up and Dad's given up and now you've given up, too."

"I didn't say that, Slim."

"No, but it's the truth, isn't it? You don't think he'll get better no matter what anybody does, so why bother doing anything?"

"Slim, you've got it all wrong. The idea is he'll do better

at home, don't you see? If this is where he's happiest—if this is where *he* wants to be. Because it's really his decision, honey. Nobody else has a right to tell him how to—"

He breaks off there.

So I finish for him. "How to die," I say.

"Oh, honey," says Larry, reaching for my shoulder, "I'm sorry. I didn't mean—"

"Yes, you did," I say, pulling away. "It's the truth, that's all. Why shouldn't you say it if it's the truth?"

I'm cold all over. It's maybe seventy-five degrees and the sun is shining, but there's ice inside me—ice cubes in my blood, icebergs the size of that sucker that sank the *Titanic*, smashing up against the walls of my brain.

"Slim?"

Larry wants to keep talking, but I'm too cold. If I opened my mouth, smoke might start coming out, like it does from the freezer door in summer.

So I shake my head and go to my room.

I sit there staring at this poster I have on my wall. It's a picture of a guy in a hang glider, just the blue sky and this guy all by himself up there, with nothing but one bright red-and-green-and-yellow sail that's keeping him from crashing to the ground.

I don't know what that means; you tell me.

Anyhow it steadies me someway. I'm still cold, but I'm steadier now. And after a while I'm steady enough to leave my room and set the table like always. I fill the water glasses and I help carry the serving dishes to the table, and then I sit there pushing the food around my plate while my dad pushes his around his.

"You're quiet tonight, Slimderella," he says. "Are you feeling all right, honey?"

I tell him I'm fine, just sort of tired is all, and he nods and pats my hand.

I can feel Larry looking at me, but I don't look back.

After supper I sit between the two of them on the green couch and watch television until my dad's head starts to nod. It's early yet, but we all say good-night anyway and go to bed.

But I don't go to sleep. I lie there in the moonlight, staring at my hang-glider guy, stuck forever in midair.

Frozen in time.

I lie there waiting until the house grows quiet, no water running or doors closing or toilets flushing anywhere, nothing but a low hooting from an owl that comes around sometimes out my window, and the *tick tick tick*ing from the kitchen.

I get up and put on my slippers and my robe and walk in there, stepping soft and easy. Sister is sleeping on her pillow near the stove; she looks up and thumps her tail, but I put my finger to my lips like Dad always does, and she stays where she is. "Good girl," I whisper. And then I open the cabinet in the pantry where Larry keeps his toolbox and take out everything I need: three screwdrivers of different types and sizes, all carefully labeled and numbered. That should do it, I guess.

The cat clock is too high up for me to reach. I have to get a chair and stand on it, then climb from that to the counter by the stove, so I can take it off the wall.

Sister is watching me the whole time.

"Don't look at me like that," I whisper as I climb back down again. "You're a dog, remember? You're supposed to hate cats."

Thump, thump, thump goes her tail.

But she keeps on watching. She watches me all the time I'm unscrewing the cat's back and taking out the batteries, and the screws that hold the springs that hold the batteries, and the little metal thingamabobs that hold the screws, and the coils and gears and wheelies and I don't know what all else—everything that will come out, comes out.

I gut the damn thing is what I do.

And then I put all the guts in a paper lunch bag, and I put the bag in an old milk carton in the bottom of the trash can, and I climb up again on the chair and the counter and hang the empty cat back on the wall.

In my bedroom, the guy on the hang glider is still right where I left him, frozen in blue sky.

Don't let go, bud, I think at him as I pull the covers close around me. Whatever you do, don't let go.

The house is so quiet, I don't shut my eyes all night.

15 ✳

IF IT WERE anybody but Larry, I'd think he just hadn't noticed that the cat clock has stopped ticking. If it were my dad, say, who never looks at clocks, loses every watch you give him, is always surprised when somebody tells him how late it's getting—I mean, Dad just doesn't have that little gizmo or whatever it is in the brain that makes a person *understand* about time, you know? It's like he exists outside of it somehow, like the passing of minutes and hours— even days—isn't really connected to him in any way that matters.

But this is Larry I'm talking about here—Larry who has only been late once in his whole life, Dad swears, and that was when his old apartment burned down, and he broke his foot trying to get out, and even then he only missed his appointment time by fifteen minutes. "He's just so *prompt*," my mom said about him once, and the way she was shaking her head, I don't think she meant it as a compliment. And as for that cat clock, I bet he double-checks his watch against it eighty or ninety times a day at least. Only once do I remember there being anything wrong with it—it had slowed down a teeny bit is all—and when it turned out the batteries were low, Larry had them out of there and new ones put in before you could even say boo.

So I know he knows, even though it's four o'clock the next afternoon and he still hasn't said one word about it. I can *feel* him knowing in the air all around me—in the careful way he asked how I slept this morning at breakfast, in the extra radishes and double-fudge brownie I found in my lunch bag at school, in the white around his knuckles where he was gripping the steering wheel when he drove me home just now.

But he hasn't said a word, and neither have I. I mean, I would say yes if he *asked* me; I wouldn't *lie* about it, for pete's sake. But it's not so easy, just bringing it up out of the clear blue sky, you know? *Excuse me, Larry, pass the pepper, please, and by the way, I smashed that wonderful clock that your dying mother left you.*

Then again maybe he's just distracted by the earthquake.

It wasn't The Big One or even bad, really, but those things always make everybody sort of jumpy—"nervous and twitchewy" is the way my dad says it. There you are lying in your bed or whatever, and all of a sudden there's this grumbly rumbling noise coming out of nowhere and everywhere, and everything's rolling around under you, and the blinds are jiggling, and the lampshades are shaking, and that glass of water you left on the dresser is dumping out into your shoes. And then it's over before you even have time to wake up all the way or remember what it is they taught you to do in that earthquake preparedness class at school: *Oh, yes, I was supposed to brace myself in a doorway or*

*at least put the blankets over my head in case the window cracked
to pieces, wasn't I? Well, maybe next time . . .*

That's how the quake early this morning was anyhow—
just a five point four on the Richter scale, they said on the
news, with the epicenter way off in the mountains somewhere, where it didn't do any harm. Not even a big enough
rattle to wake my dad, though Larry was knocking at my
door less than a minute later and asking if I was all right,
which of course I was—I mean, earthquake-wise, at least.
I had only dropped off to sleep as the sun was coming up,
which couldn't have been more than five minutes before the
shaking started; anyway that's how it felt.

But here's the weird thing: we keep having these little
aftershocks, you know? Just babies is all they are—not even
enough to make the pictures hang crooked—but you'll be
walking along, and the earth will give this strange little
shudder under your feet, like maybe you would feel if a
train rattled past in a city a mile underground. Or not even
as big as that—more like you're standing on some huge
animal's back, and it just reached over to scratch its toes—

No, that's still not right. I'll tell you what it makes me
think of. It's like that picture of Father Time that I saw once
in a fairy book when I was a little kid: Father Time, who's
like this unbelievable giant, you know? With a long white
beard and all. And he's sleeping in some enormous cave
that's way down deep in the earth. And he's snoring, you
see, and stirring in his sleep—maybe having nightmares or
something, maybe even getting ready to wake up like he
does in that old story, remember? When the world is about
to end?

Anyway it's getting to be late afternoon, and I guess I

ought to start on my homework, but I can't concentrate. My eyelids feel like they're made out of sandpaper, but I'm too tired to sleep, too prickly to lie down, too nervous and twitchewy to keep still. Meanwhile Dad is sitting by the window with the baby's blanket in his lap, nodding off again, and Larry is across the room at his overhead projector, fooling with some kind of layout for a fishing magazine, I think. His work looks like the worst kind of dull to me, but he usually seems to enjoy it pretty well. Most days when he's in there you can hear him humming while he draws, even though he couldn't carry a tune if his life depended on it. It's just this little music-free murmur he makes—"Like a bee buzzing in clover," Dad whispered to me once, waving me over to hear. "That means he's happy." And then we stood there grinning and listening, being careful not to let Larry see us—"Because he'd be embarrassed," Dad said, "and then he'd stop." And afterward he made me swear not to ever mention it.

Which was fine with me—I mean, I really don't give a durn whether Larry hums or not, except that sometimes it kind of gets on my nerves. But today—well, he's *not* humming is the thing; he's in there with his forehead all knotted up, and he's dropping pens and wadding up paper and cussing under his breath, which isn't like him at all. And I can't help thinking it has something to do with the stupid clock, you know? And with what we said to each other yesterday, and with my dad, of course, and maybe with something else. I don't know what it is, exactly, but the air's all wrong in here, and the earth keeps shuddering, and I wish whatever it is that's going to happen would *happen*, for crying out loud. I wish somebody would say *something*—

"Slim—would you come in here for a minute, please?"

Larry's voice startles me so, I jump about a foot in the air.

"Sure," I say, taking a deep breath. *Okay, this is it then. He's going to let you have it for the clock. But what do you care? Just tell him you'll pay for the damn thing, that's all. . . .*

I walk in and sit down at the old dining room table, but he's already pacing and shaking his head. "No, let's go in the kitchen," he says. "It's quieter there."

So I say sure and follow him into the kitchen, even though I don't really hear any difference. Maybe he just feels safer surrounded by all his pots and pans, I don't know, or—

Or maybe he doesn't want Dad to know what we're saying?

I'm getting cold again.

I sit down stiffly in one of those hard ladder-back chairs we've got in there, because suddenly my legs feel all rubbery, but Larry goes to the sink and rinses out a glass and wipes off the faucet and flips the water on and off again for no reason that I can see. And then finally he turns around and says in this voice that's much too quiet, "Look, Slim, in a way this isn't any of my business—"

So don't say it then.

"But in a way it is, you see. In a way it's my only real business, the only thing that matters to me."

This isn't just about the clock, is it?

It's my turn to say something, but I can't—or won't. I don't anyhow. And after a moment he says:

"I'm talking about your dad, Slim. About what's best for him—and for you, too, honey. What's best for—for all of us."

Including you, you mean.

Another pause, and then he goes on:

"And it seems to me that this strain—well, it just—it's not fair to you, that's all. And I think if your mother realized what you were going through, she—"

"My mother doesn't have anything to do with any of this," I say quickly, standing up; my tongue and my legs come back to life at the same time. "You leave her out of this, Larry!"

"Slim, we can't leave her out of it. She's your mother. She has a right to know what's going on."

"That's not for you to decide. You're not my dad. You're not—" You're not anything to me, I start to say, but I catch myself somehow. I've got to calm down; I can't let him think I'm going crazy or he'll call her, I know he will. "Please, Larry, I'm okay. I won't be any more trouble to you, I promise. I'm sorry about the clock. It was a stupid thing to do, but I'll get it fixed. I'll pay for it—"

"Forget the clock. The clock doesn't matter. It's you that matters, Slim—you and your dad, don't you see? Don't you see that's all I care about?"

"Then don't call my mom. If you care about us, please don't call her. Please—I need to be with my dad, Larry. He wants me here; he told me he does. I couldn't stand it if he—"

"Hey, guys." It's Dad, standing in the doorway with Sister, looking anxiously from me to Larry and back again. "Everything okay?"

For a split second there's the guiltiest pause you ever heard. And then—

"Sure, Mack, everything's fine," Larry says. "We were just—just trying to decide about supper, that's all. Slim thought maybe pasta and—well, how does pasta sound to you?"

"Sounds great," says Dad, putting his arm around me. He's leaning—oh, so lightly—on my shoulders. "Whatever the lady wants."

Larry just stands there for a moment, studying the two of us, like we're a puzzle that it's up to him to solve. And then he clears his throat, and nods a little, and starts opening cabinets. "Pasta it is," he says quietly.

✳

BUT AFTER supper I'm looking for a ballpoint on his desk, and there's his Rolodex turned to my mom's address and phone number. So I tear out the card and stuff it in my pocket, and I swear even while I'm doing it I feel another one of those growly little rumblings under my feet—old White Beard having nightmares again.

Well, hell.

I guess I could smash every last clock in the world and it wouldn't make a bit of difference, would it? Because the truth is, that ticking hasn't stopped at all.

It just keeps getting bigger, I think as the hot tears start pushing against my sandpaper lids. Bigger and bigger and bigger and bigger, and there's nothing anybody can do. . . .

And then all of a sudden there's this terrible pounding on the front door and the doorbell ringing at the same time, and even as I'm running to answer it, I can hear Isaiah's voice calling from the porch: "Slim? Are you there? Hey, Slim, hurry up, it's me!"

"What's wrong?" I ask, throwing the door open. Larry and Sister are right behind me, and Dad is hobbling after them in his baggy old pajamas, his face creased with worry lines.

And I'll be dogged if the kid isn't standing there beaming like he's just won the lottery, hugging an old yellow newspaper to his chest.

"Good Lord," I mutter, "are you crazy or what?"

Isaiah holds out the paper with trembling hands and answers me with a question:

"Ever hear of the Miracle Man?"

16 ✳

"THE *WHAT*?"

Nobody has moved an inch. Larry and Dad and Sister and me are all just standing here staring at the saucer-eyed prophet on our front porch and wondering whether or not to call the Wacko Wagon.

"The Miracle Man," Isaiah says again all in a rush; he's out of breath, like he's been running. "He's got this health-food place up in the mountains—well, in the valley, really, the Hungry Valley, they call it—and you can go up there, and they have these Dragon Trees all around it, and if you cut them open you get—"

"For crying out loud, Isaiah, come on inside if you're gonna tell us a whole story. You're letting all the cold air in."

Which sort of wakes up Dad and Larry. "Sure, come in, come in," they say together, and, "Is that your mother out there in the car? Tell her to come in, too."

"Naw, that's not Mama, that's my aunt. Mama's not supposed to drive till after the baby now, so Aunt Alva's staying with us for a while. She wanted frozen yogurt, so she said she'd give me a ride. She's out there eating it."

"Oh," says Larry, looking sort of overwhelmed by this boatload of information. "Well, it is a little chilly tonight. I'll just go out and see if maybe she'd like to bring it in here."

So he leaves, and it's up to my dad to be the host, pajamas and all. "Well, how you been keepin', Isaiah?" he says with a grin, leading everybody into the living room. "It's been a while, buddy. Great to see you."

"Great to see you, too, Mr. Mack. We were all real glad to hear you were home from the hospital." Isaiah must be pretty shocked at seeing how bad my dad looks—I mean, I'm here every day, and sometimes it still shocks me—but I have to hand it to him, he covers it up real well.

"Thanks, son. It's good to be home."

Dad's smile is so sweet and his blue eyes are so sparkly even under all that swollen crud that I have to swallow hard real fast and growl at Isaiah, "So what's all this about a—a—what did you call this guy?"

"The *Miracle* Man," Isaiah says, handing me the newspaper. "Just look, it's all in here."

But before I have a chance to do more than glance at it, Larry and Aunt Alva come inside, and then there are all the introductions to go through: Hello, I'm Angelina's big sister, it's wonderful to finally blah and blah, and, I've heard so much about such and such, and, Sorry about the pajamas, I'm afraid my robe is in the wash, and, Oh, no, not at all, we shouldn't be barging in like this, but Isaiah said it was sort of an emergency and that we couldn't phone ahead for some reason—

He's looking at me kind of guilty and grinning at the same time. "Had to show old doubting Thomas in person. She'd never believe me on the phone."

"Oh, Isaiah," says Aunt Alva, shaking her head at her crazy nephew and sounding mortified. She's tall like Angelina and almost as pretty, just older and a little thinner; that frozen yogurt would probably be good for her, but I guess she's left it in the car. Also she's sort of more anxious looking, probably due to these two deep lines denting her forehead from in between the eyebrows up. "Well, I do apologize for disturbing you like this, but Angelina had gone to bed early, and this child was all worked up, weren't you, Isaiah? Said there was some kind of message?"

"What message?" I ask him.

"That's what I've been trying to tell you!" he says, and his big eyes are blazing again just like that. "The newspaper—I mean, the way I found it—I don't hardly believe it myself! I was just sitting there watching TV, see, and all of a sudden Gabe—you remember Gabe—"

"Gabriel," I explain to Dad and Larry. "That's the bird."

Isaiah nods and rushes on: "Right—our myna bird. He's been kind of grouchy lately, I don't know why; he just won't say a word for some reason. And anyway all of a sudden I'm sitting there, and he says, 'Clean my cage.' Well, I don't pay him any mind at first. I'm kind of busy with this show I'm watching. And then he says it again—'Clean my cage.' And still I don't move. I just say, 'Okay, Gabe, as soon as "The Fresh Prince" is over.' See, that's why my dad taught him to say that, because sometimes we sort of forget. And so then I'm back to watching, but old Gabe, he's starting to get restless now. He's ruffling his wings and scooting back and forth on his perch like he does, and then he starts up with 'Hello, Isaiah.' And I say, 'Hello, Gabe, just hold on a minute, will you?' But Gabe, he won't shut up now. He's back to 'Clean my cage, clean my cage, clean my cage' until I can't stand it anymore. 'All *right*,' I tell him, 'I'll *clean* it!' "

Isaiah stops for breath there and smiles that smile, like he's said something wonderful.

Meanwhile we're all pretty much just staring at him.

"So that's *it*?" I ask. "That's the message?"

"Wait," he says, sounding all mysterious. "That's not the best part yet."

"Oh," I say, sighing. "So what's the best part?"

"Just *listen*," he says. "So anyway I'm a little mad at Gabe for bothering me like that, but I get up and go look in the storage room for some fresh newspaper to put at the bottom of his cage. That's what we always use, see, so we keep it stacked up in there. And sometimes we get around to recycling, but mostly the stacks just keep getting bigger and bigger. Some of it goes back a couple years even. And I guess I'm maybe moving too fast or something, because I'm still thinking I can get this over with and see the end of my show. And anyhow I kind of jerk the door open, and this whole big pile of papers comes crashing down on top of me. So now I'm *really* mad. I'm cussing old Gabe and trying to get those papers piled back up in a big hurry, but you wouldn't believe what a mess. And then right in the middle of all that—well, this one here just sort of *jumped out* at me, you know? I mean, I look down and there it is in my lap: *Miracle Seekers Flock to Site of Unexplained Phenomenon*, and this big picture of God's face staring right up at me!

With all the crutches thrown down under it and the sick people getting cured and—well, once I see what it's all about, it just *comes* to me, you know? That this whole thing is a message, and I'm *supposed* to see it! I mean, you tell me, what are the odds against a thing like that happening by *accident?*"

For a moment there's nothing but dead silence. And then—

"A million to one," my dad says softly. I stare at him in surprise; he's not *buying* this stuff, is he? But the look on his face—well, it's not as if he's lost his mind like Isaiah or is making fun of him or anything; it's more like—well, more like *respect* somehow. Like he remembers how it feels to believe in something that hard.

Anyway Isaiah beams at him, but meanwhile everybody else is looking pretty embarrassed. Aunt Alva says, Well, my goodness, Isaiah, that's real interesting, but we really ought to let these poor people get to bed, and Larry says, Oh, no, not at all. But I notice he doesn't say a word about this big message, he just wants to know if they need any help getting rid of all those old newspapers. And while he and Aunt Alva are talking about recycling bins, Isaiah is busy showing me and Dad the rest of the article, telling us everything about the Water of Life and the Dragon's Blood and the Face in the Mountain and all. And I'm trying to be polite and not say a word about how sad it is that he's finally tumbled over that edge he's been teetering on ever since we met way last January. Who knows, maybe it was all that rain soaking into his head.

"I'm gonna talk to Ms. Crofford about working up a trip," he's saying, still moving his mouth a mile a minute as Aunt Alva is doing her best to drag him out the door.

"We could use the church bus, I bet—just drive up there next weekend, you know? The paper says it only takes about an hour and a half if you don't hit any traffic. We could be back the same day easy."

"Uh-huh," I tell him, waving good-bye. Then they're finally gone, and me and Dad and Larry and even Sister are just standing here looking at one another, like, What was *that* that just blew through here, a whirlwind or what?

"Well," says Larry, "he certainly has a lot of energy."

"He's nuts, is what he is," I say.

And Dad chuckles at that, but he's still got that funny look on his face. "Oh, I don't know," he says, staring out the window at the car's disappearing taillights. "It might be a nice little trip at that. It's supposed to be pretty up that way this time of year."

Good Lord. He wants to go, doesn't he? He really wants to go!

But Larry is shaking his head. "I don't know, Mack. That's kind of a long drive, don't you think?"

Dad doesn't answer; he's worn out just from this one little visit and has to be helped even on the short walk down the hall to his bedroom. Which is maybe an answer right there, come to think of it.

But I keep puzzling over that look on his face when I'm lying in my bed, rattling around with the latest aftershock, still too tired to fall asleep. And I'm wondering, what is it about Isaiah's crazy story that would get my dad interested like that? Okay, sure, I guess it is pretty weird when you think about how Gabriel talks in Isaiah's daddy's voice and all. It's even creepy in a way—a message from a dead man, coming out of a bird's yellow beak. But *that* message? I mean, come on, Isaiah—"Quoth the raven, *'Clean my cage'*"?

Still, there was something there that got my dad thinking. It couldn't be all that God stuff, could it? Not that he doesn't believe in God—I mean, I guess he does; his dad was a preacher, as a matter of fact, and we still go to church sometimes. But we never really talk much about any of that. It's all so kind of embarrassing, you know?

Well, actually there was this one time we *sort of* talked about it. It was a couple of years ago, when I was still living in Texas, and Dad flew home for Mom's and his high school reunion, because naturally he's still friends with about a million people there, too. And anyhow one day he was driving me in his rental car out to see our cousin Frankie, and we happened to go past the cemetery where his folks are buried.

"Maybe we ought to stop by for a minute," Dad said. So we picked up some flowers at this little shop that's right across the street—"Conveniently Located" it probably says in the yellow pages ad—and took them over to the graves. And then Dad put the flowers down, and we just stood around for a while, feeling kind of weird. I don't remember exactly what we said at first except that we couldn't help noticing the part of the plot that was reserved for him—his name and everything but the final date all carved in the headstone already. Grandpa liked to plan ahead, he said; Larry would have loved him.

But as for this being his final resting place, Dad said no, thank you, when his time came he'd rather not be stuck in a little box like that.

"Just burn me up and scatter me around. I always liked to travel."

"Oh, Dad," I said, sort of laughing. Back then the idea of him dying was the farthest thing from my mind.

But not from his, I guess, because after that he got kind of quiet.

"Do you remember my daddy?" he asked me. (He didn't ask about his mama, because I never knew her at all; she died when he was still a kid.)

"Not very well," I told him. "Mostly from pictures, I guess."

That seemed to disappoint him some until he thought it over. "Well, you were just a little thing when he had the stroke—not even five yet. I don't guess you remember what you said the day he died?"

I told him no.

He smiled a little then. "The two of you were great friends. You thought he hung the moon. And then when he was in the hospital so long, not able to speak or anything, you used to worry about him just lying there. You said he hated it, as if he had told you he did. So when I came home that day and explained that he had gone to heaven, your face lit up like the sun. 'Now he can fly!' you said."

Well anyhow, that's how Dad put it to me. I don't really remember saying it at all. I don't remember ever believing any of that stuff, to tell you the truth; seems like I always figured it was all just fairy tales. But the way my dad told that story—well, it was like he thought it mattered, you know? Like it meant something to him.

Of course after that he got to joking, like always, telling me about his actress friend Hilary who wants her favorite review carved into her headstone: "Her tall, slim good looks served her well." And about Dylan, the comedy king, who wants his to say: "Mr. Baker gets better and better with each performance, and in this part, he is adequate."

"And then of course there's my own *personal* favorite,"

Dad went on, "which I think would be most appropriate, under the circumstances."

"What's that?" I asked.

He closed his dancing eyes and crossed his arms like a corpse. "As Captain Von Trapp, Hugh McGranahan the Third lends new rigidity to an already wooden role."

We laughed all the way to Cousin Frankie's.

But that look on his face tonight—I can't stop seeing it, you know?

As for Isaiah—well, I think I understand what he's doing. The president was kind of a disappointment, right? So now he's going up one step higher—just moving on up the chain of command, you might say. Which is his own business, of course, even though that's bad enough; the crazy kid's just setting himself up for another big letdown. But now it looks like he's got my dad stirred up some way, too, and as sick as he is—well, it worries me, that's all. Because the way I see it, if God's really the one in charge around here, He's got a lot of explaining to do.

And with Him, you don't even get form letters.

17 ✳

THE NEXT morning I wake up mad. I don't know why or even who with, exactly, just mad, like somebody declared war overnight and handed me a helmet. I have to pick a side is all.

The *opposing* side, that's the one I want. The side where everybody else *isn't*.

It starts at the breakfast table, with just me and Larry sitting there; Dad was too exhausted to get out of bed this morning. Small wonder, what with crazy people busting in here at ungodly hours, and then the earth refusing to keep still. It's getting so nobody can sleep with all these damn aftershocks. They shook me awake three times in the night, and afterward my heart was pounding, so I lay awake for hours. And then finally after the third one I fell into that deep sleep that's like a black hole you just can't climb out of, you know? I can still feel the shadow of it slugging around inside my head like that awful cold medicine I had to take last month, making me stupid. So now I'm groggy and stupid and mad all three, and when the phone rings, it's almost more than I can do to answer it.

"Hello," I mutter, knowing who it is already.

"Hey, Slim, it's me. The trip's on! We're going next Sunday, okay?"

"No," I answer, louder than I have to, and Larry jerks his head up to see what's wrong.

"What do you mean, no? Just go ask your dad. I know he wants to go—"

"No," I say again. "He's still asleep. He's worn out, Isaiah. He was only being polite last night, that's all. No way he can drive all the way up there and back. Anyhow who knows if the place is even there anymore. That newspaper was two years old, in case you didn't notice."

"Sure I noticed. I called 'em already first thing this morning. They're still open and everything."

"First thing this morning, and they *answered*? Good Lord, Isaiah, it's not even seven-thirty yet!"

"Oh, that didn't matter. Those health-food people get up at the crack of dawn. They're just feeling too good to stay in bed. And anyhow he was *right there*, Slim—the Man himself. I *talked* to him! I told him there'd probably be fifteen of us driving up for lunch next Sunday, and he said fine, he'd write it down in his book."

"Fifteen? Fifteen *people*?"

"Well, sure. Me and Mama and Aunt Alva—she's not letting Mama out of her sight till the baby gets here, she says—and Ms. Crofford and Roberto and Suzannah and Duke and Lorraine and all their relatives, of course, and then you and your dad and Mr. Casey—"

"*No*, Isaiah, didn't you hear me? My dad's not well enough."

"But that's why he *has* to go—that's why he *wants* to go, don't you see? I mean, what's he got to lose? It can't hurt to try, Slim. The worst that can happen is it doesn't work, right? And if it doesn't, well, so what? You're back where you started, just one day older, that's all. What's one day compared to a whole lifetime?"

"Look, I can't talk now, Isaiah. I'll be late for school. Just forget it, okay? Go without us—I don't care. It's your business if you want to waste your time chasing after some phony miracle, but I said *no*, got that?"

"But, Slim—"

"*No*, Isaiah."

A pause. And then:

"Well, that's okay, you don't have to decide right now. I'll talk to you after school. Maybe I can get Aunt Alva to drop me over there—"

Good Lord. Is he deaf or what? I wonder as I slam the phone down.

"Isaiah?" asks Larry, looking at me across the table.

I nod and stab at my pancakes. Why does he bother asking when he already knows the answer?

"It's good you didn't encourage him," he says, reaching for the syrup.

For some reason that irritates me. He just sounds so damn *sure* of himself, you know? So I can't help myself, I say, "Why?"

"Why what?"

"Why is it good I didn't encourage him?"

Larry looks puzzled. "Well, because—because we can't go, like you said. You were right to say no."

I shrug. Don't ask me why. I just shrug, that's all.

Which makes him nervous, I guess, because then he says, "Anyway the whole thing's probably a fraud.

116

I only hope Isaiah isn't *too* disappointed when he gets up there."

"How do *you* know it's a fraud?" I ask. Or maybe it's not me, really; it's this demon that's crawled up out of that black hole in my brain and perched on my tongue, saying things I never planned.

"Oh, come on, Slim—you said it yourself—"

"I know what I said. I said Dad's too sick to go, that's all. I didn't say the whole thing was a fake."

"Well, maybe not in so many words, but surely you don't mean that—"

"Don't tell me what I mean, Larry. You don't know what I mean. You don't understand anything."

"Well, maybe not, but—" Larry throws down his napkin; he's looking pretty frustrated now. "Oh, for heaven's sake, Slim, what are we *arguing* about? I was *agreeing* with you, remember?"

One beat, maybe two, while this sinks in. And then I hear myself saying:

"Yeah, well, maybe I was wrong."

"What?"

"Maybe I was wrong, that's all. I mean, who knows, Isaiah could be right. Like he said, it's just one day. What do we have to lose?"

"Your dad," Larry answers. He's frowning now. "We have your dad to lose."

That knocks the demon right off his perch; for a moment he can't say a word. Meanwhile Larry is looking at me. And then finally he asks:

"Why are we fighting, Slim? What's wrong?"

I grit my teeth. "Nothing's wrong. I just—well, I just

117

started thinking about Dad, that's all. I mean, we're sitting here deciding everything for him, when he's the one who ought to be saying whether or not he wants to go. And you heard him last night, he said—"

"Oh, for pete's sake, Slim, he was just talking, that's all. He said he'd like to fly up to New York for the Tony Awards, too. He said he'd like to see the leaves change in New England. He said he'd like to visit the Eiffel Tower just once in his life—did you know he's always wanted to go to Paris? But we're not going to do any of those things either, don't you get it? Because he's sick, Slim. He's just too sick."

Larry gives his plate an angry shove on that last word. I guess he only meant to push it away from him, but it knocks into his glass of orange juice and that goes crashing onto the floor; the racket of shattering glass fills the room. For a moment neither of us moves or says a word. We're just sitting here, looking at each other. The only sound is the *drip, drip, drip, drip* of juice from the table ledge. And I know he's mad, and I know he's hurting, but I don't care; the demon won't let me care. I'm too mad myself, and my throat aches.

"I wish it was you," I mutter. "I wish you were the one that was sick."

Still Larry doesn't move—not a muscle, not a hair. And then he makes a weird little exhaling noise, something between a laugh and a sob, if that's possible. "I wish I were, too," he says. "Dear God, I wish I were, too." And he stands and starts cleaning up the mess.

✳

I DON'T apologize. I know it was a terrible thing to say, but I can't help it. I can't say the words *I'm sorry,* because I'm not. I'm glad I hurt him. He hurt me, too. What right does he have saying what my dad can do and not do? Who does he think he is? I'm still mad is the thing, but at least I'm not cold; mad is better than cold. And it's easier than sorry any day.

I guess Larry's still mad, too, because his mouth is closed tight all the way to school. And even when he picks me up in the afternoon, he doesn't say a word; I get in the car and slam the door, and we ride home like a couple of strangers, not even from the same country—a taxi driver and a customer who don't speak the same language.

I guess I should be afraid that he'll call my mother, but I'm not. Not anymore. Because I'm not leaving anyway. They can't make me leave unless they tie me up and drag me away, and even then I'd just turn around and come back. I'd steal money for the bus ticket if I had to. I'd hitchhike. I'd walk on bloody feet like the animals in all those dog and horse stories.

Larry's the one who ought to leave. He's not even kin to us. I can take care of my dad by myself; we'll get along just fine.

I want to go sit by Dad on the couch when I get home. I want to just sit there with his arm around me and watch the freaks on "Oprah" or "Geraldo." But he's sleeping again, and I don't want to be in the house with Larry so I go outside. I figure I'll climb up the hill in back and maybe let the wind cool my face off a little. All day it's been burning up almost like I have fever, which I don't.

But the hill is harder to climb than it used to be. Larry has planted this weird stuff all over it—ice plant he calls it. He says it's supposed to protect the house from mud slides and brush fires like we get around here sometimes. There was this guy on the news last fall who claimed it was why his house was the only one in his neighborhood that survived the last big disaster, so Larry rushed right out and bought enough to carpet the county. It's terrible, if you ask me, like something from another planet—all thick leaved and spongy and slippery looking, not pretty at all. My shoes slide around in it, and I fall hard on one knee, but I pick myself up, and finally I get past the vile green junk. I make it to the little rock ledge at the top of our property, which is as far as I can go.

There would be a great view of the mountains from up here—if there *were* any mountains.

There's no wind either, not even a breeze, nothing but good old L.A. lung rot and the sun beating down, making the sweat run along my neck and my arms in grimy little rivers. But at least I'm alone, just me and a couple of bored-looking mosquitoes who aren't even interested enough to bite. They may not be the best company in the world, but right now I prefer them to most humans I know.

At least nobody knows where I am.

"Hey, Slim! Are you out here?"

Oh, no, not Isaiah—

"Slim! Hey, Slim!"

Maybe if I don't say anything, he'll go away.

"Oh, *there* you are! Whatcha doin' up there, girl? Aunt Alva dropped me off while she's shopping and—well, hold on a minute, I'll come up!"

Well, hell.

He scrambles up in nothing flat, like he was born walking in ice plant, and plops himself on the rock beside me.

"So did you decide yet? Did you talk to your dad? Are we going on Sunday or what?"

120

I shake my head. "It doesn't matter what I decide. Larry says we're not going."

"But your dad—"

"It doesn't matter what my dad wants. The king has spoken, so now we all have to bow down and do whatever he says. And if he says we're not going, we're not going."

"Oh," says Isaiah. I expect him to go back into his same old song and dance, but that's all he says, just "Oh."

Which irritates the heck out of me for some reason.

"What do you mean, 'Oh'? Aren't you gonna tell me how we're making a terrible mistake? How we *have* to go?"

"No," says Isaiah. "I guess not."

"You guess not? Well, *why* not, for crying out loud? Wasn't it only this morning you were going so crazy on the phone?"

"Well, that was just you I was talking to, Slim. You never mentioned that it was Mr. Casey saying your dad couldn't make it. And he's the one who's really taking care of him and all. So he would *know*, wouldn't he?"

I try to stay calm. I mean, I know it with my head— what are we arguing about here anyway? A stupid trip I didn't want to take in the first place, remember?

But the demon won't let me stay calm.

"He doesn't know anything," I growl. "If it wasn't for him—well, things would be different, that's all."

"Different how?"

"I don't know, just *different*, okay?"

Isaiah gives me a funny look. "You don't mean—naw, you don't mean *that*."

"What?"

"You don't mean you think any of this is *Mr. Casey's*

fault, do you? You don't think this virus is anybody's *fault*. . . ."

One of the mosquitoes is buzzing in my left ear now. I slap at it and shrug. "I don't know," says the demon. "Maybe."

"Aw, Slim"—Isaiah's big eyes get bigger—"you don't mean that. That's like something one of them skinheads would say!"

"Well, what if it is?" The words spit out of my mouth like poison; I'm so mad now I can't even see straight. "Just leave me alone, Isaiah. Quit telling me what I mean. I'm sick of people telling me what I mean. I'm sick of Larry, and I'm sick of Miracle Men, and I'm sick of you!"

Isaiah just looks at me, peering deep with those terrible eyes. He shakes his head a little, like he's never been so disappointed in somebody. "You don't mean that," he says again, so quietly I can barely hear him.

And then he climbs down the hill through that icy green crud and leaves me alone like I wanted.

18 ✳

MY DAD is awake when I finally come in from the hill.
"What's wrong, honey?" he asks the minute he sees me.
"Nothing, I just—I just have a lot of homework," I tell
him.

"Oh," he says. "Poor baby."

But he doesn't look convinced, and dinner is pure tor-
ture, like one of those endurance tests they give you in
swimming lessons: how long can you do the dead man's
float before you start to sink? There's Larry over there
working on his strong, silent routine, and here I am trying
not to gag on my mashed potatoes—did he put in the lumps
on purpose?—and there's Dad in between us, doing his best
to make conversation. But I can't hear a word he says
because there are too many other voices playing inside my
head like some garbled tape recording:

I wish it was you. I wish you were the one that was sick—
Aw, Slim, you don't mean that—
Don't tell me what I mean—
That's like something one of them skinheads would say—

Shut up, Isaiah, I'm not listening to you! Just shut up, do you hear me?

I jab my fork into my asparagus stalks and chop off their heads, one by one. I try humming the theme from "Jeopardy!" and reciting the times tables. I count every lemon on the tree out the window. But it doesn't do any good—the tape won't stop; even after I go to bed it keeps playing:

I wish it was you. I wish it was you—

Like something one of them skinheads would say—

No! It's a lie. I'm not like them. I'm nothing like those guys—

Nothing? Nothing is all some people around here have done—

I won't listen. I *won't*. I turn over and turn over and turn over again. I cover my ears with my pillow. I wrap it around my head like Madame Angelina's turban, but still they won't shut up:

You don't think it's Mr. Casey's fault, do you? You don't think this virus is anybody's fault—

Well, what if it is? Just leave me alone. I'm sick of people telling me what I mean—

Aw, Slim, that's like something Felix Howard would say—

Felix Howard? Good Lord, I haven't thought of Felix Howard since the third grade—

But he was the first, remember?

Suddenly I'm eight years old again.

I'm eight years old, and I have to be an angel in the Christmas pageant at Sunday school. I tell Mama about it, but this is the year she's marrying what's-his-name, Bob. So she keeps putting it off and putting it off, and finally, right before they leave for their honeymoon in Reno, Nevada, I come in while she's packing and say it one more time: "But what about the wings?"

And she gets this guilty look on her face and says, "Oh, honey, I forgot. I'm so sorry. But listen, it will be all right. Your daddy can help you with them."

Well, that makes my stomach hurt, or maybe I just have a flu bug or something, but anyway I say, "Okay, Mama, y'all have a good trip." But on the inside I'm thinking, Oh, no, Daddy doesn't know the first thing about wings.

And that's how it seems at first.

"Wings?" he says to me, looking blank. He and Larry have come to town to stay with me the whole two weeks that Mama and what's-his-name, Bob, will be gone. And I couldn't be gladder, except for this one complication.

"Angel wings," I explain with sorrow. "Big ones, you know, like they have."

"You're going to be an angel?" he asks, leaning in. "Which one?"

"The Angel of the Lord," I answer, apologizing.

"The Angel of the Lord?" he repeats, and his face lights up. "Why, honey, that's a *lead*! Well, sure, you've got to have *real* wings for a part like that!"

And he's so excited now that I can't help but start feeling better. Then he and Larry take me over to Padilla's Flowers and Unique Gifts for Special Occasions, which is run by Dad's friend Miss Pat, and next thing you know we're coming home with our arms loaded full of peacock feathers and ostrich plumes in every color you can imagine and some you might can't, and we're gluing them onto these long sticks and crinkly papers that are really meant for kites, I suspicion, and Dad is singing "Hark the Herald Angels" in his Alvin and the Chipmunks voice and making me and Larry laugh till it hurts, except for when he has to stop and cuss some on the hard parts. And then they get a sheet and double it over and make me lie on it on the floor, so Dad can cut it out around me in an angel dress shape, and finally after some more cutting and cussing and both of them sticking their fingers while they take turns sewing it all together, we're done.

And I am one amazing-looking angel, with wings to die for.

"Good God Almighty!" says Mary Fay Aldine when I show up at dress rehearsal. "Where'd you get *those?*"

I don't blame her for being jealous. "My daddy made 'em for me," I say, feeling kind of proud and shy at the same time.

Mary Fay crinkles her nose like maybe she's about to cry, and I notice that her wings are nothing but tacky white cardboard with pitiful Magic Marker squiggles for feathers. So I figure I should soothe her hurt feelings, and I say politely, "Yours are real nice, too, Mary Fay."

That's when she busts out laughing.

"What's so funny?" I ask. But Mary Fay just babbles, "N-n-nothing," and backs away across the stage over to where Charlotte Colgate is flirting with King Herod and a couple of Wise Men. And pretty soon they're all over there giggling behind their hands and glancing my way.

Well, by now my cheeks are starting to burn, but I still can't figure out what in the heck is the matter with everybody. Maybe I've got a dang rip somewhere, I think, checking myself up and down. But everything seems okay, and I'm just getting ready to go ask the gigglers if they've lost their minds or what when I catch sight of Felix Howard prissing up his lips real silly under his Wise Man mustache and pointing down into the audience. So I follow his finger with my eyes, still looking for the joke, and what I see is

Daddy and Larry, sitting up all proud in the front row, waiting for the rehearsal to begin.

"The fairies have landed," comes Felix's snide whisper.

Which is right where my memory starts to blur.

But the way my dad tells it later, ours is probably the only nativity show in town that has the Angel of the Lord punching out a Wise Man at the top of act one. . . .

How can he make us laugh when it's all so awful?

He has to make us laugh, honey. That's his sword and shield, don't you see?

All around the mulberry bush, the monkeys chased the weasel—

What are trucks doing inside the carnival? I must be dreaming—

I'm there now. I can see it all over: the balloons and the merry-go-round and the laughing crowd, with my dad right smack in the middle, shining like the sun itself on all those pale little moon faces. And then all of a sudden the picture goes dim, and there are bottles breaking and little kids screaming and maniacs shaking their fists and those clumsy black trucks screeching off into the dark. . . .

There's this one guy hanging on in the back—the only one I get a good look at. He's a pug-ugly little cuss, all angles and elbows, with flapping monkey wings and a terrible tail and a mean little monkey face, and he's grinning the awfullest grin I ever saw. But wait—I've seen that face somewhere, haven't I? And those wings—why, just look at them—peacock feathers and ostrich plumes and—what's that the monkey's saying?

I wish it was you. I wish it was you. I wish you were the one that was sick—

"No!" I cry out. "It's a lie—that's not me!"

I'm awake now. I'm sitting up in my bed, and I'm sobbing as if my heart would break. It feels like it's broken already.

"Slim? Honey, what's wrong?"

It's my dad. He's here. He's switching on the light and holding me in his arms and rocking me back and forth—"It's okay, baby, it's okay. You were having a nightmare, that's all."

"Oh, Daddy, I'm so sorry, I'm so sorry. Tell Larry I didn't mean it. I never meant it—"

"Meant what, sweetheart? There's nothing to be sorry about. It was a dream. It's nobody's fault."

But Larry is here, and he knows what I mean. He's standing in the doorway, listening. And when he hears what I'm saying, he comes over and sits beside us, and there are tears in his eyes, too. "It's okay, Slim. Everything's okay."

"I'm sorry, Larry—"

"I'm sorry, too, honey."

"But you—you never—"

"I was upset. I said some things—we were both upset, that's all."

Sister is here now, too, pushing her wet nose under my dad's hand, wanting to get in on the comforting.

"Oh, for heaven's sake, Sister, don't tell me *you're* having nightmares?" Dad asks, scratching her behind the ears.

And that makes us all smile. I'm starting to calm down now.

But still Dad and Larry don't leave me. They sit talking quietly while Dad strokes my hair, waiting for my breathing to smooth out. And it feels so good, and suddenly I'm so tired; I'm almost drifting off when I hear him say, "Maybe what we need is a change of scenery."

Larry is quiet for a moment. And then he says slowly, "Well, it's not such a big trip, really. I guess the fresh air would do us all good."

Dad nods and closes his eyes—he's starting to drift himself—but Sister gives him another nudge. And he smiles and takes her silly old dog face in his hands and looks at Larry. "Toto too?"

I'm half-asleep again as I hear Larry sighing. "Sure, Mack," he says softly. "Toto too."

19 ✳

SO ANYHOW we're going. And now it's coming up daylight Sunday morning, and I'm still lying here waiting for that alarm to start ringing. Sort of like I used to do at Christmas, except this time I'm not hoping for a new bike or a Barbie with automatic hair or anything like that. Just a nice day and nobody hurting too much and a good lunch that my dad will be able to swallow and maybe keep down for once. Plus Father Time taking a dose of Sominex or Nytol or whatever it is he needs to hold the ground steady under our feet for the next twenty-four hours—I wouldn't mind adding that to my list. I know Isaiah is hoping for a lot more, and don't get me wrong, I'll take whatever miracles they're handing out. But after all the carrying on around here lately, I guess a nice little trip with no worries for a few hours would be miracle enough for one day.

Dad starts coughing again along about sunrise, but he seems better by breakfast. When I join him at the kitchen table, he's sitting up pretending to eat his Cream of Wheat and smiling his party smile.

"Good morning, glory," he says. "All set for the mountains?"

"*What* mountains?" I tease him, because they're not back yet. I guess the special-effects people are off on spring break or something, because the sky here is its usual L.A. sort-of blue, but it's still too hazy to see much of anything up north.

Dad grins. "Just you wait, Thomasina. Just you wait."

"Everybody about ready?" It's Larry, coming in from the driveway, where he's been loading up the car with enough maps and bottled water and emergency equipment to get us to Siberia and back. He's going to have to unpack it all and switch it over to the minibus when we get to the church parking lot; Ms. Crofford got that all worked out just like Isaiah wanted. The pastor almost said no because of insurance or some such until Larry offered to drive; he's had his chauffeur's license ever since college, when he drove a school bus to help pay his way. But I suspect that he would have run out and gotten whatever he needed to be in charge, no matter how much trouble it was, because the truth is he wouldn't trust anybody else to get us all up there and back safely.

"Just about ready," says Dad. "Have to slip into my wig, that's all."

Larry grins kind of sheepishly and shakes his head. "Oh, Mack, you don't have to wear that old thing. It was a terrible idea, I know."

"Are you kidding?" says Dad. "I *love* that wig!"

Which I'm sure is the gospel truth, considering all the mileage he got out of it last time.

So Larry goes and gets it for him, and pretty soon Dad's got the poor dead critter on his head again.

"All right," he says, peering out from under it with the old crazy-happy sparkle in his one good eye; that bad lesion has the other one just about completely closed now, so it looks like he's winking all the time. "I'm ready for my close-up, Mr. deMille."

And we're off. Or almost anyhow. There's a bit of a delay while Larry fixes a stuck gear on this wheelchair he's rented for the day—or at least that's what he tells my dad, with the excuse that it might be nice to have it handy, "in case anybody gets tired."

There's just a heartbeat of a pause, when I can feel my dad hating the sight of the damn thing. He knows as well as Larry does that it's here to stay.

And then he nods.

"Good idea," he says. "You know how cross Sister gets when she's on her feet all day."

❈

EVERYBODY gets to the parking lot at about the same time.

"Hey, Mack!"

"It's Mack!"

"Good to see you, Mack!" a half dozen voices call at once.

"Howdy, folks!" he says as Larry helps him out of the car. "Is this where we catch the stage to Abilene?"

"Oh," breathes Lorraine when she sees Sister, "is this your dog?" Looks like she's catless for today.

"Yes, ma'am," Dad says with a grin. "Sister McGrana-han in person. She said to me, 'Mack, I want to go meet that nice Lorraine girl you keep talking about.' So here she is."

Lorraine smiles shyly and kneels right down for a doggy kiss.

"Hello, Slim," says Ms. Crofford. "It's good to see you, sweetheart." She's standing bright faced by the bus, even though Isaiah told me on the phone yesterday that she hadn't really been all that thrilled about coming. She was worried about building up false hopes and such. "Sometimes in this life we have to make our own miracles" is what he said she said. But then the group took a vote, and she finally agreed, as long as everybody promised to think of the trip as being strictly for pleasure—a nice outing, nothing more.

But that's not the only thing that comes to my mind when I look at the lady.

"Good to see you, too," I murmur, and my cheeks go all hot again, remembering the dumb scene with Suzannah.

But Ms. Crofford and the others—even Suzannah herself—must have had a meeting about how to handle rotten apples; anyhow they're busy pretending it never happened, which I appreciate.

And as for Isaiah—"Oh, I knew you didn't mean it" is all he ever said about that day on the hill, when I tried to apologize on the phone.

"Hey, Slim!" he's hollering now. "Come see this bus— we got a CB and a rear-window defogger and everything!"

"Don't you go messing with any of those buttons, Isaiah," Aunt Alva calls after him. Her worry dents are deeper than ever, I believe.

But Angelina is her usual sweet self, just as calm as sunshine. "Hello, honey," she says, giving me a hug, and at the same time the baby kicks at me—straight from her stomach to mine—giving me that peculiar little flutter again. And we both laugh, but I can't help seeing that she's looking tireder than ever and—well, puffier, I guess is the word for it, kind of bloated, you know? Not just big and beautiful and pregnant.

But there's no time to worry, because Larry is already hustling everybody into the bus, which says ALL SAINTS EPISCOPAL DAY-CARE CENTER on the side.

"Okay, folks, time to go! Want to try to get ahead of that weekend traffic!" Which is crazy, it seems to me, since we *are* the weekend traffic—I mean, how can you get ahead of Sunday on Sunday?

But anyhow we all pile in, and next thing we know we're hitting the road. The sun is shining, and our little yellow bus is heading out the Hollywood Freeway, past the Church of Scientology Celebrity Center and the Capitol Records building and a hundred thousand palm trees, then over to the Five and north at last toward those slippery hide-and-seek mountains.

"I feel like we ought to be singing camp songs," my dad jokes. And everybody smiles, but nobody takes him seriously, because the group's mood is different today, not gloomy or anything, but quieter than at the carnival. Quietly hopeful, I guess that's about right—because of it being the Lord's day, maybe, and us out to track Him down.

Plus we're all six weeks older now.

So when we hear the *blam!* and feel the *bumpeldy jerk!* of a tire blowing, everybody stays calm.

"Don't worry, folks, no problem," says Larry, pulling over to the shoulder like an expert and hopping out with his toolbox, which he's brought along just in case whatever they've got in the bus isn't good enough.

He sounds almost cheerful—which I guess makes sense when you think about it; I mean, if you're one of those people who prepares for every conceivable calamity, it would probably be a little disappointing if *nothing* went wrong.

"Can we help you with that, Mr. Casey?" Duke's dad—followed closely by Duke himself—says happily. Then of course we all have to get out so they can jack up the bus, and the men stand around looking manly and discussing lug nuts and tire irons while Larry does the changing.

"Nice work there, Old Woolly," my dad tells him, clapping him on the back when he's done. And then we all climb back in, and the little bus cranks up again.

"How much longer before we get there?" Isaiah asks. He's got his old newspaper spread out on his knees, studying the map that's printed next to the picture.

"An hour, tops," Larry calls back. "We'll probably be just a few minutes past our reservation."

That's when Ms. Crofford taps him on the shoulder. "Excuse me, Mr. Casey. I'm sorry to bother you, but is that smoke coming out from under the hood?"

"Smoke?"

There's a shade less spring in Larry's step as we all climb out a second time. "What in the—well, would you look at that mess!" He's got the hood up now. "That guy who checked the oil at the gas station didn't get the dipstick back in right, see there?"

We look. Sure enough, there's oil spattered all over the place, sizzling in angry-looking little beads on everything in sight, and black smoke hissing out of the engine.

"Oh, no!"

"I can't believe—"

"Well, why in the—"

"Didn't the oil light ever—"

"So *now* what do we do?"

"Don't panic," says my dad. "I'll bet we have extra oil in the back of the bus, right, Larry?"

But Larry is shaking his head. There are two ropy-looking tendons standing out on either side of his neck. "Not enough," he says grimly. "This thing'll take four quarts at least—maybe five. I guess we'll have to call triple A."

"Good grief—"

"But that means—"

"Will we have to go back, Mr. Casey?"

Lorraine looks close to tears again, and Isaiah's worry dents are as deep as Aunt Alva's.

"Oh, no," says Dad before Larry can start nodding. "Those guys'll have us fixed up in no time."

No time turns out to be an hour and a half.

"How much longer before we get there, do you think?" Duke asks when we're finally back on the road.

"Forty-five minutes, tops," says Larry.

"Will they hold our reservation?" Aunt Alva asks.

"They have to," says Suzannah. "I'm starving! Isn't everybody starving?"

Everybody says yes. Everybody except Lorraine, that is, who is sitting in the back of the bus now with her face buried in Sister's coat.

"Excuse me, Mr. Casey?" says her mom. "I'm sorry, but could you please pull over again for just a minute? Lorraine says she's going to throw up."

The trip from hell, my dad whispers in my ear. He's teasing, naturally, but he's starting to look pretty haggard, and some of the other sick people are keeping mighty quiet:

136

Suzannah's sister has her head in Suzannah's lap, and Roberto is trying to get a window open so his brother can get some fresh air, and Angelina is leaning back with her eyes closed while Isaiah fans her with his newspaper.

"Maybe we should go back," Aunt Alva worries while we're waiting again.

"Oh, no—"

"Not *now*—"

"But we're more than halfway there!" says Isaiah. "We can't go back now!"

"Why don't we take a vote?" says Ms. Crofford as a white-faced Lorraine and her mother climb back aboard.

The vote is twelve–two—Aunt Alva and Larry are the two, with Ms. Crofford abstaining—in favor of pressing on.

"After all," Duke's dad says cheerfully, "bad luck is supposed to come in threes, right? I think we're already past the legal limit."

"I wish he hadn't said that," says my dad.

But everything seems okay for the next half hour. Dad is napping beside me, and according to Larry's calculations we ought to be there in another fifteen minutes, tops.

"When do we start seeing the mountains?" Suzannah asks.

"Any minute now, honey," says Angelina, opening her eyes. "This old haze will clear just as soon as we get a little farther away from the city."

But the haze isn't just regular haze, after all.

It's fog.

"Fog?" says Larry. "In the middle of the day?"

"You never know in the mountains—"

"Didn't anybody check the weather?"

"Who checks the weather in southern California?"

"Larry does," says my dad, opening his eye. "What did they say today, Larry?"

Silence.

"Larry?"

"I forgot to check," he mutters.

Dad starts humming the theme from "The Twilight Zone."

"Oh, well," Angelina says quickly. "It's bound to burn off pretty soon. Fog never lasts much past noon."

I wish she hadn't said that. . . .

A half hour later it's worse than ever, the thickest stuff you ever saw—like the wool from Dad's crochet basket, only without the holes. It's rolling down in ghostly waves from what must be the sides of mountains, but I couldn't swear to it; I mean, I *think* we're in them now, but we still can't really see them. Traffic has slowed to a crawl mostly, though every now and again a huge shadowy truck goes roaring around us.

I almost can't bring myself to look at the drivers, for fear of what might look back.

"Shouldn't we have passed the turnoff by now?" Isaiah asks anxiously, checking his newspaper for the hundredth time.

Larry shakes his head. "I don't think so." He's hunched over the steering wheel, squinting into the blank white screen of the windshield. "It's so hard to see in this stuff—has anybody spotted the sign for Gorman?"

"No, look, Mr. Casey—I'm sure you've passed it. See here, that says Lost Hills next junction. That's way past!"

"Well, hell," Larry mutters. "We'll just have to take

that and double around on that little back road they show on the map. See the one I mean?"

"Yes, sir," says Isaiah. "That should work."

A half hour later we're still doubling back, I guess—doubling back and winding around and climbing up and up and then coming down again for no apparent reason. And now the sturdy little blacktop road that started away from the highway like it knew exactly what it was doing has dwindled away into gravel and sand, and then—all at once—it stops altogether at a huge pile of rocks that looks to have slid out of nowhere.

"The earthquake must have been worse up here," Duke says quietly. But nobody else says a word. All us saints in the day-care bus are just sitting here staring at Larry, waiting for him to tell us what to do.

"Well," he says finally—it sounds like his jaws are clenched—"there has to be a way around. We'll just have to go back to that fork in the road we passed a while back, that's all."

But that fork leads to another rocky washout, and by now we've turned and twisted and doubled back so many times that we've lost the highway altogether.

"I change my vote," says Suzannah at the third dead end. "I want to go back, Mr. Casey."

"M-me, too," Lorraine hiccups.

"Maybe somebody's trying to tell us something," says Roberto.

"Fine, then," says Aunt Alva. "Let's go back."

"Good idea," Larry says. And then he adds in a growl, "If I only knew where back *was*."

"I think I remember this episode," my dad says under

his ragged breath. "The one where they all wake up fifty years older."

"Mr. Casey?" says Suzannah. "My sister has to go to the bathroom.

"Oh, Lord, can't she wait? We're out here in the middle of nowhere, and—well, you're not desperate, are you, honey?"

"Pretty desperate," says the sister; they're the first words I've ever heard come out of her mouth.

"Me, too, I'm afraid," says Angelina.

"Me, too," say a half dozen voices.

"You're *all* desperate?" Larry sighs. "Well, we'll have to find some bushes, then. No telling when we'll see a service station."

So we all pile out of the bus one more time. Or almost all anyway.

"Can you make it, Dad?" I ask, but he's too exhausted to move.

"No, baby, I'll be fine here. But I guess you'd better take Sister."

"Don't anybody go too far! Keep within sight of our headlights!" I can hear Larry's voice calling from behind me as I strike out looking for some kind of cover. Not that it matters much with this chilly gray stuff blowing all around us; it looks as if we're all wrapped in shrouds, like dead people in horror movies.

"Try to stay together!" Larry is yelling now from somewhere up ahead. "Or—well—as close as possible anyhow...."

That's funny. Wasn't he just *behind* me?

"Roberto?" calls his brother's voice. "Where are you?"

"Mama, I'm over here!"

"Where's Isaiah?"

"No, Lorraine, stay with me, honey—"

"Sister? Sister, get back here, for crying out loud—"

"Dad?"

"Duke?"

"Come *back*, everybody—this is no time to be modest. You're all going way too far!"

Good Lord, what a mess—

"Sister, I said *come back*!"

What time is it anyway? Three, four o'clock, who knows? You can't tell in this dismal stuff; we might as well be on Mars at midnight. Or on the moon, maybe—is that where we are? Stumbling around on the dark new moon, with nothing but earthshine to go by?

"Lorraine? Where are you, honey?"

"Roberto, I'm over here!"

Are the other voices getting fainter?

"Sister?" I try again. "Come on, girl, we've got to go back."

Except like Larry said, where *is* back anyhow? I can't even make out the headlights anymore. . . . Shoot, if I ever see that fool myna bird again, I'll—

"Ouch! Oof! What in the heck is—"

"Hello?" says a woman's voice. "Who's out there?"

"It's me, Slim!" I call back, hugely relieved. "Is that you, Aunt Alva? Watch out, there's some kind of bad sharp stuff over this way—feels like swords—almost just put out my eye."

"Oh, I'm sorry," says the voice—*is* that Aunt Alva?— and now I can see a light flickering, too—a flashlight, I guess—and a hazy form moving toward me. "Just come on around to your left, sweetie. It's safer over here. By the way, is this your dog?"

I can make out the speaker a little better now: not Aunt Alva, after all, but an old gray-headed lady in what looks like a polka-dot robe, with her hand on Sister's collar.

Who on earth—?

"Yes, ma'am," I say as soon as I get over my surprise. "I don't know what got into her. She never runs off like that."

"Oh, well, bless her heart, she just got turned around in this terrible fog, that's all. Poor little thing, it's a wonder the pair of you didn't come up blind or stabbed through the heart, one, with these awful old Dragon Trees all around. I *told* my son he ought to get rid of 'em, but he won't listen. He's stubborn just like his—oh, my goodness, you're shivering! You just come on inside and warm up, sweetheart, and I'll take my flashlight out to the road for the rest of your party. I *thought* those were headlamps we saw! But of course we could hardly believe it in this weather, and coming up that awful back road, too—how on earth did you ever find your way?"

It takes me a moment to locate my voice.

"Did you say Dragon Trees?"

20 ✳

THE MIRACLE MAN Natural Food Emporium and Traveler's Rest is a little brown house (at least as far as I can make out in this gray goop) nestled deep in the Hungry Valley. Once we get past the Dragon Trees—big ones and little ones and every size in between—we can see its lights, winking at us through the mist.

"Well, my goodness, all of you just come right in and get the damp out," the old lady is saying as she ushers in our dazed-looking group. "Why, you're all white as sheets. Aren't you feeling well? But then naturally you're exhausted after a trip like that—imagine you getting up here in this nasty weather! Oh, yes, sir, you just let that nice dog come in. She's a good girl, isn't she? Such a pretty thing, too. I hate to see her out in that mess. I guess it's probably against some regulation, but I don't think it would hurt just this once. This fog almost qualifies as an act of God, wouldn't you say?"

Nobody answers; we're all pretty much just standing here, still in shock. So the old lady goes right on:

"Oh, my, and here's a little mother-to-be! Oh, you poor

child—you come sit right down, sweetie, and the rest of you, too. You see, we have the big table all ready. My son told me he had a group down for lunch in the book, but when it got so late we thought, well, of course, you couldn't possibly make it on a day like this. I told the cook to go home an hour ago, I'm afraid. But don't you worry, I'm younger than I look, and Lord knows I can still find my way around a kitchen!"

"Your son, did you say?" Ms. Crofford manages to ask as the rest of us fall into our chairs.

"Well, yes, sweetie, he's the one that runs the place. I don't ordinarily work here, you see. I'm just helping out for a few weeks till he gets on his feet again."

"On his feet?" Ms. Crofford repeats, looking doubtful. "Is he sick?"

"Oh, no," says the old lady. "He just had a little accident a few days ago, nothing too serious, thank the Lord."

I look at Isaiah, but he won't look back.

"What kind of accident?" asks Larry.

"Oh, well, just a bit of bad luck, that's all. He was up on the mountain, fixing some damage that last earthquake did to the Face, you see—which is kind of peculiar, considering it was a quake a few years back that had put it there to begin with. And anyway while he was on the ladder, we had one of those aftershocks, and poor Buster fell off and broke his leg. But he's fine now, just taking it easy. He's upstairs this minute watching 'The Family Feud,' see there? Right up in the little loft behind that tacky old beaded curtain. I keep telling him it's time to redecorate, but you know how men are when they get used to things."

There is a moment of deep silence. Not *dead* silence, exactly, since now that she's pointed it out, I can hear the

144

drone of a TV from above our heads, where a shadowy figure is seated. But deep—so deep you could throw a rock in it and never hit bottom at all. And then:

"The Miracle Man is named *Buster?*"

It's my dad asking. He's sitting in that wheelchair Larry thought of, thank God; otherwise I guess we would have had to carry him in from the bus.

The old lady chuckles. "Well, no, sir, his real name is Franklin Arthur Wise, Jr. But when my husband was alive, we always called him Buster to set the two of them apart, you see, and I guess it just stuck."

"Oh," says Dad. He's squeezing my hand, trying desperately to keep a straight face. I can feel him tensing every muscle in his body, *commanding* himself not to laugh, for poor Isaiah's sake.

"And what about you folks?" Mrs. Wise goes on. "I guess you came up for the scenery? Well, isn't that too bad, and it's so nice this year, too! The flowers turned out in a real good show, the best I can remember. You know they're saying it's due to all that rain we had earlier—what was it they called that? *El Pinto* or some such? Oh, no, listen to me, I believe I've got it mixed up with those ships in the history books. . . ."

"*El Pinto, El Niño, and El Santo Mario,*" my dad says under his breath. He's about got the circulation squeezed out of my hand by this time.

Isaiah himself has been fearfully quiet up to now, just sitting there like a rock, taking in one piece of bad news after another. But now he speaks up in a small, strained voice:

"Buster was—fixing the Face?"

Mrs. Wise sighs. "Oh, I told him he oughtn't to go up

145

there, but he wouldn't listen. He still has this idea the Face is going to bring in business, I guess. 'Buster,' I said to him, 'those days are long gone, thank the Lord.' Of course, we did have quite a bit of interest in it a couple years back—well, after that first quake, you know. It was all because of an article they ran in one of those offbeat L.A. papers. I doubt you would have seen it. Oh, it was such a to-do—they sent up a photographer and everything. But I saw that picture later, and, you know, I believe they had touched it up. They thought it made for a better story, I suppose. Personally I don't approve of that sort of thing, and in his heart of hearts Buster doesn't either. I can't think why he agreed to go along with it. It was just hard times and that old devil greed that got to him, I'm afraid. But surely after all this trouble—I mean, the fall, of course—he's bound to have learned his—"

A change comes over Mrs. Wise's kind old face; all at once there's a look of terrible comprehension dawning there. I guess she's just now taking in the full meaning of Dad's wheelchair and Suzannah's sister's wheelchair and the poor wasted faces and figures of half the people at the table, not to mention the old yellow newspaper that Isaiah's got clutched to his chest. "Oh, dear," she murmurs, putting two and two together at last, "you don't mean to tell me—please don't tell me that these poor sick folk have come all the way up here because of that old *article?*"

"Well, just partly—" Ms. Crofford begins.

But Mrs. Wise isn't listening; the truth is looking right at her, in Isaiah's big disappointed eyes. And so she turns to the shadow behind the beads upstairs and cups her hands to her mouth. "Do you hear that, Buster? All these poor sick folk out on a day like this, just because of that silly article! I hope you're ashamed of yourself!"

Buster doesn't say a word, but I guess he must have a remote control for his television, because suddenly the volume goes sky-high: *"Survey says, forgetting to cut your toenails!"*

"Pay no attention to the man behind the curtain," my dad whispers. There are tears sliding out of his eyes.

And Larry must be struggling for some kind of control himself, because all of a sudden he stands up real straight and pats my dad's shoulder. And then he starts speaking in that gruff bear voice. "Well," he says, "this is all really interesting, ma'am, but these people are hungry. Do you think we could—"

"Oh, certainly. Oh, my, yes!" says Mrs. Wise. "Oh, my goodness, yes. What have I been thinking? You all just take a look at those menus there, and I'll see what Buster has in that kitchen. The cook won't let me near it as a rule—you know how particular these health-food people are. But to tell you the truth, I've been dying to take a peek. Lord knows what peculiar brands I'll find."

Larry's eyebrows shoot up. "Well, uh—excuse me, Mrs.—uh, Mrs. Wise? If I could be of any—well, that is, since your help is all gone—"

"You want to pitch in, sweetie?" she asks, beaming him a motherly smile. "Well, isn't that the nicest thing! Why, certainly, you just come along with me. I'm too old to be passing up offers from handsome young men. At my age, I'll take all the help I can get."

So Larry follows her, and Ms. Crofford and Aunt Alva go, too, and the rest of us just keep sitting here, trying to

hold ourselves together and act normal for Isaiah's sake—
like this is how we *always* spend our Sundays.

"You okay, buddy?" Dad asks, and Isaiah shrugs and
says, "Oh, sure." We all know he's lying, but we don't let
on; we're managing our parts like champs until Mrs. Wise
and her helpers come back in with our water glasses. And
then, while they're still going around the big table and filling
the glasses from shiny blue pitchers that have "The Water
of Life" printed on their sides in old-fashioned gilt letters,
Dad takes a little sip of his and right away starts coughing.

"Oh, dear," says Mrs. Wise, rushing over after Larry,
who is already pounding him on the back. "Are you all
right, sweetie?"

"Fine," Dad sputters when he's finally got his breath
back. "Just fine—sorry, everybody. . . ."

But Mrs. Wise is shaking her head. "Well, goodness,
I'm the one who's sorry. It's this water, that's all. I keep
telling Buster he's got to have regular pipes put in and get
rid of that old well. 'Buster,' I told him, 'you have to face
facts, son. That water has grit in it.' "

Good Lord. For a moment we just look at one another.
And then my dad's mouth starts to quiver, and his eyes
crinkle, like maybe he's going to start leaking tears again.
"The water has grit in it?" he repeats hoarsely. "There's
grit in the Water of Life?"

That does it. He just can't help it; he can't hold in his
laughter for another second. It gushes up out of him in
hoots and wheezes and coughs and great guffaws that shake
his poor frail body like a giant's hand drying out an old
dishrag. And Larry and I aren't any better; we've caught it
now, too—we're holding on to Dad and to each other and
laughing that terrible hurting laughter that feels so awful

and wonderful together that there's nothing you can do and no way to stop it. "Dear God," Dad keeps saying, "there's grit in the Water—there's grit in the Water of Life. . . ."

And now the others are all laughing, too. I look at Isaiah, worrying even while I'm hysterical, but he's in his mother's arms, and they're laughing and crying at the same time and leaning on Aunt Alva, who has collapsed in the nearest chair and is rocking back and forth, holding her sides and letting forth great whooping belly laughs and looking helplessly at Ms. Crofford, who has also lost it. She's chortling and chuckling and every now and again coming out with one of those awful unladylike snorts that I'm guilty of myself, together with Duke and his dad and Roberto and his brother and Suzannah and her sister and Lorraine and her mom and even Mrs. Wise, who is laughing right along with everybody else, covering her mouth with both hands and just tittering away, like she's understood the joke from the first. And meanwhile Sister bounds from chair to chair, smiling her dog smile and giving out short happy barks and licking everybody in sight. All of us just a mess, in other words, just a roomful of helpless gigglers, in actual peril of our lives, if it's true you can really die laughing.

I can't say for sure how long this goes on—quite a while, I guess, because it seems like every time a few people start to calm down a little, my dad will say those six little words again: "G-g-grit in the Water of L-life!" And we're right back where we started, worse than ever. But finally we're all pretty well worn-out; our jaws are aching, and our noses are running, and we settle down enough to wipe them and our eyes, both, and begin remembering how hungry we are. But I guess that laughter is a kind of magic, because we don't even mind the pain in our empty bellies so much anymore, or maybe it's just okay to be hungry when you know that supper is on its way. It's all right now, that's all I know; everything is all right again. And so we sit here eating crackers—"The best crackers I ever put in my mouth," Aunt Alva swears—and sipping on some kind of sparkling berry drink that Mrs. Wise has uncovered somewhere, since nobody trusts the water now, and talking real loose and easy about the whole crazy day, and laughing some more—only softer now. And finally when the food comes out steaming hot and piled high on big platters, it's such a meal as I've never eaten in my life and scarcely dare hope to again, this side of paradise. I don't know some of the mystery ingredients, maybe, but I recognize chicken and fresh corn and beans and avocados and leafy green lettuce and those good ripe tomatoes that shouldn't be in season at all right now but here they are anyway and basil and olive oil and soft mozzarella and squash and brown rice and cream of potato and some kind of spicy lentil soup and hot bread with butter melting and three kinds of pie for dessert.

If there's seaweed, it slips right by me.

"Delicious," my dad keeps saying. "Absolutely delicious." The truth is his taste buds haven't worked right in months, but, you know, today I almost believe him. I mean, he actually manages to eat most of his soup and even a bite or two of everything on his plate—not near as much as most of us do, sure, but what amounts to a whole feast, for him.

The other PWAs seem to be making out real well, too, thank goodness. Lorraine's mom is all sweet smiles, and I actually hear Duke's dad asking for seconds on the rhubarb pie, and Suzannah's sister has the most color I've ever seen in her cheeks. She's even talking quietly to Roberto's brother, who has scribbled her phone number on his napkin. And as for Isaiah's mom—well, she's still looking a bit tired; she's leaning back in her chair with her eyes closed, but there's a gentle expression on her face, even so, like she's glad just to be sitting there, listening to the sound of everybody's contentment.

Isaiah himself is quieter than usual, but not like before, when his disappointment was still so new to him. I guess he's made some kind of peace with it, now that the day has turned out all right in most other ways. Of course we've still got to make that long trip home, but at least all the tires look okay, and the dipstick's back in place, and we'll be heading out on the right road and—

"Well, isn't that nice," says Mrs. Wise, lifting a corner of one of the white curtains she's had shut against the gloom ever since we arrived. "Looks like that fog's clearing up, after all."

"Really?" says Larry, jumping right up to see. "Well, thank goodness for that. It'll make the trip back so much—"

He stops short as he arrives at the window; there's something out there that's made him gasp and forget what he was saying. "Good God," he whispers, just loud enough for me to catch the words. "Will you look at that?"

"Look at what?" I ask, and I get up to join him while Dad says, "What's wrong, Larry? What is it?"

"Nothing's wrong." Mrs. Wise chuckles. "He's just had his first look at the real California gold, that's all."

As she's speaking, she's drawing back the curtains the rest of the way and flinging open the big bay window that's behind them. And all at once the room is filled with light, the most wonderful light I've ever seen—not only from the sun but from the earth itself, which isn't anything like the soggy gray world it was two hours ago. It's all turned to colors now, to every color you can imagine—not just gold, though there's plenty of gold, but green and blue and purple and red and even chartreuse and burnt umber and—

"Every color of the rainbow," my dad says under his breath as Larry pushes his wheelchair over to the window.

"Oh, my . . ."

"Oh, my Lord . . ."

"Have you ever seen . . ."

". . . anything like it?" everyone is murmuring at once; for some reason nobody seems capable of speaking above a whisper.

Except Mrs. Wise, who just can't stop chuckling over her pleasure at seeing us all so stunned. "Well, I *told* you, didn't I? It's a real nice show this year. But now don't waste time in here—we can settle up the bill later. You all ought to get on out *in* it while you still have this good light! Lucky it's daylight saving time or you'd have lost it long since."

So we do what she says, not moving too quickly because that seems wrong—don't ask me why, exactly—like running in church somehow. Anyway we just sort of ease out the door, like dreamers afraid of waking. Wheeling Dad and Suzannah's sister before us, we walk past the Dragon Trees and into this big beautiful field of flowers that stretches all the way to the mountains—

And stand there amazed, like it says in the song, wondering how did we get into heaven?

"Poppies," Mrs. Wise explains as Sister gives a joyful bark and goes leaping after invisible rabbits. "Cups of gold they call them. And of course there are all sorts of other flowers mixed in—Indian paintbrush and avalanche lilies,

152

and those pretty blue ones are kin to the Texas bluebonnet, I believe."

"Boz," my dad whispers.

Larry leans over him anxiously, not hearing him just right, I guess, or thinking he's so tired he's talking crazy.

"What, Mack? Do you mean the movie? We'll be going home soon, honey. We can watch it then—"

"No," I explain, looking at my dad's shining face. "He means we're there."

And that's what it's like, all right. Only we're not just *over* the rainbow, we're *in* it. And it's in us—in us and around us and through us—it's under our feet and in our eyes and blowing its sweet breath into our lungs. It's stretching out before us for mile after mile after mile, then spilling its brightness even onto the mountains themselves, turning them into great glorious mounds of color—tie-dyed mountains, that's what they are. Like nothing I've ever seen, nothing on *this* planet, surely—and yet looking so right, so *familiar*, that I can't help thinking maybe this is how it's been all along. My eyes just weren't open, I guess.

"Is it still Sunday?" Lorraine whispers, and that makes everybody smile, but I know what she means—it feels as if we've been on this trip forever, for our whole lives, even. I thought it'd be dark for sure by now; I thought we didn't get into the restaurant until close to four. But for once—for just this moment—time seems to have stopped altogether.

"It's still Sunday, sweetheart," my dad says quietly. "The Spirits have done it all in one day."

"Spirits?" Lorraine seems puzzled.

But I look where he's looking, up there in the mountains, and I think I can see what he means.

Mrs. Wise is looking, too. "You know, when that article

first came out, there were quite a few people who came up here searching for the Face," she says, putting her arm around my shoulders like we're the oldest of friends. "And of course once they saw it, most of them pooh-poohed and went away disappointed. It just wasn't enough like their picture of it was the problem, not like what they were *expecting* at all. But you know what I think?"

Lorraine shakes her head.

"I think it's all in the eye of the beholder. Why, some mornings I wake up and that Face is nothing but a pile of rocks, and nobody can tell me any different. But every now and then—when the light's just right, and the shadows hit just so—well, like now. Can you see there? Why then, I could almost swear those old sweet sorrowful eyes are looking right *into* me."

Nobody says a word.

But the rest of the group—even Isaiah—is nodding, and now *their* faces are shining like the sun.

And Dad takes my hand in one of his, and Larry's in the other, and we all lift our eyes and look back.

21 ✳

THE LAST THING we do before we start the long trip home is buy a little Dragon's Blood.

"You sure about that, sweetie?" Mrs. Wise says to Isaiah as he's standing in front of me at the cashier's counter with his red Velcro wallet in his hand. "I believe you'd do just as well with some of that Vaseline Intensive Care lotion, to tell you the truth. That's what I use. It's real nice and doesn't have such a strong odor, particularly the yellow kind and—"

Tick tick tick tick tick tick tick tick! goes the "60 Minutes" clock, turned up full blast on the upstairs TV.

"Well, goodness, Buster, you don't have to be rude. I was only trying to make certain he wants it!"

But Isaiah says, "Yes, ma'am, I'm certain," and I say, "Me, too," so she sighs and wraps us up a bottle apiece, even though she insists on charging us half price because "they've been on that shelf so long." And then she walks us out to the little yellow bus, where everyone else is all loaded up and waiting, and waves good-bye.

"Till we meet again!" she calls after us as we head out into the setting sun. "You folks drive safely, now!"

✷

WHEN we put Dad to bed that night, he's still smiling. "What a day," he keeps murmuring. "What an incredible day."

"Incredible," Larry repeats softly as he gently lifts the wig off Dad's head. The two of us stand beside him for a moment, looking down at his peaceful face. And then Larry turns off the light, and we ease out into the hall. "It was good that we went," he says quietly.

But the next morning Dad is too weak to get out of bed. He's all stuffed up and coughing again and running a temperature.

"Just a cold," he says when I don't want to leave him to go to school. "I'll be fine, honey."

And sure enough, he's a little better later. "The fever's come down some," Larry tells me when he picks me up, and by the time we get back, Dad is sitting up in his bed, half-awake—or half-asleep, I guess, depending on your point of view; his one good eye is sort of open anyhow. "Hey, guys," he croaks, smiling. "Don't I know you from somewhere?"

"Lawrence P. Casey, at your service, sir," says Larry, and he sits down beside him and begins dipping a washrag into a basin of cool water and sponging Dad's face and neck.

Dad chuckles a little under his poor rough breath. "Unforgettable," he murmurs. And then he shakes his head, like there's something else he wants to say.

"What's unforgettable, Dad?" I ask, thinking he needs help.

But he's dropping off again already, and meanwhile Larry is smiling a little and shaking *his* head, too.

"Larry?" I ask him softly. "What's unforgettable?"

"Nothing," Larry says, slipping a thermometer into Dad's mouth. "It's just a line from an old review, that's all."

"What review?" I figure by now I've heard all those stories, but so far this isn't ringing a bell. "One of Dad's?"

"No," says Larry. "Mine."

"Yours?" I'm so surprised, I almost forget to be quiet. "But you never—I didn't know you ever did any acting!"

"Only the once," says Larry—I'll swear he's blushing under that beard—and then he adds, "Thank God."

"What do you mean, 'Thank God'?"

"Lord," he says. "It was all so long ago. I was working tech for a little summer-stock theater up in the Berkshires. We were all just kids, really. Everybody did everything— building sets, painting scenery, whatever they needed. And there was this one show, just a crazy farce—*See How They Run*—ever hear of it?"

I say no.

"Well anyway, the day before it opened, the guy playing the bishop came down with mumps, a really bad case. And we happened to be about the same size, and they already had the costume, so they looked at me and said, 'Can you do it?' And I said sure—I had been at all the rehearsals and pretty much knew the whole show by heart. I figured, how hard could it be? So everybody rushed around and showed me what to do, and I was fine—I was great, even. After the dress rehearsal they were all patting me on the back and calling me a natural, and I was thinking there was nothing to it, this acting business was a snap, maybe I ought to try out for the lead next time. And then the next thing I knew, it was opening night, and I rang the doorbell, just like I was supposed to, and got ready to call out my first line. I'll never forget it: 'Mrs. Toop is expecting me.'" Larry pauses and shakes his head again.

"And what happened then?" I ask.

"Nothing," he answers.

"What do you mean, nothing?"

"I mean, *nothing*. Not a word, not even a sound. I walked on that stage and my voice just froze up, disappeared altogether. Most amazing sensation I've ever had. I saw all those people looking at me, and I opened my mouth, and nothing would come out."

"Ever?"

"Never. Not the whole night. I was just this—this *thing* in a black suit and a clerical collar that the other actors—the *real* actors—had to keep explaining away. They were wonderful once they realized I was hopeless: 'Oh, dear, the bishop has laryngitis, don't you, bishop? But I believe what he *means* to say is—' and 'What was that, Your Excellency? He's hiding in the *pantry*?' or whatever."

"Oh, Larry—"

"Most excruciating two hours of my entire life."

"Poor Larry." I'm trying to laugh quietly, so I won't bother Dad. "And then the review?"

Larry rolls his eyes. "I went down to the newsstand before dawn, thinking—I don't know—maybe I could buy every paper and burn them all before somebody saw it and sent a copy to my mother. I was prepared for the worst— how could that review be anything but awful? But what it said was 'As the Bishop of Lax, newcomer Lawrence P

Casey was unforgettable. It might even be said that he stopped the show, not just once, but several times.' "

"No!"

Larry chuckles. "Stopped it cold was more like the truth. But I was never so grateful."

"Unforgettable," Dad murmurs again, smiling even with his eyes closed.

"Was Dad in the play, too?"

"No," says Larry, taking the thermometer out of Dad's mouth and holding it up to the light to read it. "He was the critic."

"What?"

"Oh, he was just a kid himself, doing a daytime night-club act for next to nothing at one of those old resorts and working part-time at the local paper. I didn't meet him that summer—it was years later, at a Christmas party out here. Somebody said that was Mack McGranahan who just walked in, and I nearly choked on my eggnog. I still remembered the name from the column even after all that time. So I walked over and thanked him for saving my mother from years of shame, and he remembered me right away. 'Your Excellency!' he said—you can just imagine the look on his face. 'Praise the Lord, you can talk!' " Larry smiles again and smooths the damp cloth on Dad's forehead. "That's how we met, right, Jimbo?"

But now my dad's asleep for real.

✳

THE FEVER comes back in the night.

"It's nothing," Dad says the next morning, but this time it won't go away. A day passes, two days, but that durn red line on the thermometer never will go below a hundred and two, no matter how many cool rags Larry lays on Dad's head or how much crushed ice we slip between his poor parched lips.

On the third day Larry takes him to the doctor while I'm at school, but he's no better by the time I get home. He's worse, if anything.

"What did the doctor say?" I ask Larry the second I walk in from the bus stop.

In the pause before he answers, I can hear the sound of Dad's harsh breathing clear across the house.

Larry puts his hand on my shoulder. "Honey," he says at last, "are you sure you don't want to call your mom?"

✳

I DON'T know how to explain it, maybe it's the Dragon's Blood I put behind my ears and Dad's, before I left this morning, but anyhow I'm calm as I pick up the receiver and dial my mother's number in Louisiana.

"Hello?"

"Mom?"

"Why, hello, sweetheart, I thought that sounded like your ring, is everything all right?" she asks all in one breath.

And I say, Yes, ma'am, just fine, well, not fine exactly but better than before. And then I hear myself telling her all the things I've been keeping from her, everything I've been so frantic about her hearing from Larry. I tell her that Dad's sick again, bad sick, and that he won't be going back to the hospital anymore because he hates it so much and the doctor says it won't do any good anyway. I tell her that Larry's moved his work to the house so he can take care of him, and that now Dad's sleeping pretty much all the time, and that he's back to eating next to nothing. And then before she can gather her wits about her enough to start calling the travel agent for my one-way ticket to Shreveport, I tell her that the only reason I'm telling her all this is that Larry's right, she's my mother and she deserves to know the truth, but I'm okay and I'm staying, I need to stay, I have to stay.

And while she's still reeling and trying to think of all the reasons why I can't, I hand the phone to Larry, who has been standing right here beside me the whole time— standing here just like a rock, in case I need to lean on him. And he talks to her for a good half hour, maybe more, backing me up, saying how I'm no trouble, I'm a big help really, and how he's talked to some psychologist person— Is that Ms. Crofford? I wonder—who says that if I think I need to stay, then I need to stay.

There's another long pause, while Larry listens to whatever it is Mom is saying. And finally I hear him answer, "No, Leland, the doctor can't say for sure. A few weeks, a month, maybe. No one knows how long."

How long the dying will take, that's what he means. The truth washes over me like one of those big breakers at the beach, and for a moment it swallows me whole; I can't breathe.

But it *is* the truth, after all, and after a minute I fight my way to the top; my feet hit bottom again, and I take a deep breath and stand here listening to Larry's side of the conversation while Mom asks if she should come (he says no, please; no, thank you, Leland), and while she makes him promise to call her night or day, whenever we need her or if we should change our minds.

"Thanks, Larry," I say when it's over.

"Sure, honey," he says. Like it's nothing at all, this ten-ton weight he's lifted from my shoulders. And then he touches my cheek for just a second, and clears his throat, and hurries back to see if Dad needs anything.

22 ✳

OLD WHITE BEARD is stirring again.

The next big aftershock hits about a week later, while I'm sitting at the kitchen table after supper, trying to study for tomorrow's test on the Declaration of Independence: "We hold these truths to be self-evident, that all men are created equal, that they are endowed by their Creator with certain unalienable Rights, that among these are Life, Liberty, and the pursuit of Happiness. . . ."

That's when the rumbling begins.

Nothing too terrible, just that old lurch in the stomach while the floor comes to life, and the walls start to shudder, and the teacups rattle on their hooks behind the cabinet doors. And then it's over like always, and Larry is calling to me from Dad's room, "You okay, Slim?"

"I'm fine," I call back, starting down the hall. "Are you guys okay?"

"We're fine," he says. "Don't worry, honey."

But *fine* isn't really the word for what we are right now, with Dad slipping away from us a little more every day: every day he's weaker; every day there are fewer minutes when his one good eye is open; every day breathing is more of a struggle. Larry and I take turns staying by him pretty much all the time now; we just feel better if there's somebody close to him—somebody besides Sister, I mean. I don't know how she knows what's wrong, but she'd never leave the old braided rug next to his bed at all if we didn't force her to go outside every now and then, for fear of accidents. She won't eat or drink, either one, unless we take her food and water in there, and even then she's got nothing like her usual appetite.

"Come on, Sister," I tell her now, after I see that Dad is pretty much the same, "aren't you gonna finish your supper? Dad doesn't want *you* getting sick on top of everything."

And she thumps her tail a time or two, just to be polite, but she stays right where she is.

"What about you, Slim, did you finish·your pizza?" Larry asks. He didn't want to leave Dad even long enough to cook this evening, so we ordered in.

Fortunately the phone rings before I have to admit, "Well, no."

"I'll get it," I say, heading out the door.

It takes me a couple of seconds to realize it's Isaiah. He must have the phone too close to his mouth, or he's got his hand cupped around it or something, because his voice sounds all sputtery and urgent:

"Hey, Slim, guess where I am! It's started already—two weeks early—but Aunt Alva says that's okay, plenty of kids come early. I was three weeks early myself, and look how good I turned out."

Oh, Lord, I think as my heart comes crashing into my throat. *The baby* . . .

"Are you—is she—are they doing okay?" I stutter.

164

"Oh, sure, they're doing just fine. Dr. Bones says they're doing just fine. Mama's his prize patient, remember? Only—"

"Only what?"

There's a pause on the other end of the line, just Isaiah breathing too hard is all.

"Only *what?*" I ask him again.

"Well, she's—she's kind of hurting, Slim. She won't say it, but I can tell, you know? Aunt Alva says that's natural, that's the way it always is when babies come. It's even in the Bible or something. But I don't know, that don't make much sense to me. I mean, why would God want a thing like that? My mama ain't done nothing to *Him*—"

"Course she hasn't, Isaiah, course she didn't—"

"But she's hurting all the same, Slim. I couldn't act like I minded or they wouldn't have let me come up here, you know? You know how they do with kids—they think we're gonna throw a fit or something, tear down the place, I guess. But I wouldn't do nothing like that, Slim. You know me better'n that—"

"Course I do, Isaiah, course you wouldn't—"

"Anyhow she's hurting pretty bad, only they won't let me stay with her. Aunt Alva's in there with her because she's her coach or something, but they said I better wait out here. It's this little green room with plastic flowers on the table—ugliest things you ever saw. I wish I had some flowers like we saw on our trip. Now those were some flowers, remember, Slim? My mama sure did like 'em. If I could just get her some of them flowers right now, I bet she'd feel a whole lot better—"

"We'll get her some, Isaiah. Just as soon as the baby comes, we'll get her a whole roomful of flowers—"

"She ought to have *real* flowers, Slim. She's too good for fake flowers. Your daddy said she's like an angel, and that's what she is. She don't get mad like other moms. Some of the kids at school, their mamas are always yelling and carrying on, slapping 'em around even, but not mine, not my mama, she wouldn't do nothing like that in a million years. One time right after my daddy died and she was so sick, Aunt Alva said, Angelina, you got this baby coming, but maybe you shouldn't, honey. Maybe you ought to stop it before it's too late, maybe you shouldn't be bringing another child into the world when it might be doomed from the start. And you know what Mama said? She said, I guess we're all doomed from the start, Alva, but that don't stop us from dancing to the music while we're here. You see, she ain't nothing but good, Slim. You see that, don't you? She ought to have her some *real* flowers—"

He's crying now. I know he is. He's trying not to, but I can hear the thick sound of tears in his voice, running down his nose and dribbling all over the receiver. And here I am halfway across town the one time he needs me.

"Isaiah? Isaiah, it's gonna be all right, okay? It's gonna be all right, you'll see! Look, you want me to come down there? I could take a cab. Larry can't leave my dad right now, but I know how to do it. I'll just look in the yellow pages and—"

"No, Slim, you're just a kid. You can't be running all over this town in some taxi. What are you thinking, girl?"

"Who're you calling a kid?"

"You, that's who."

"Yeah, well—"

Before I can think of a good comeback—or *any* comeback, for that matter—another kind of idea hits me. "Listen, Isaiah, you still got your Dragon's Blood?"

A sniffly sort of pause, while he checks, I guess. And then:

"Yeah, I got it."

"Well, listen, you got to do a couple of things then. You got to get it out right now, you hear me? Out of your pocket or wherever. Okay, you have it now? Are you holding the bottle?"

There's one of those weird breathing things you do when you're starting to get over tears. Like the rhythm's all out of whack, you know? And then:

"Yeah, I'm holding it. So what?"

"You open it up—real slow, now—don't go spilling it or anything—"

"I ain't spilling nothing," he grumbles.

"Okay then, see that you don't. And don't let anybody around there see it, for pete's sake, or no telling what they'll think."

"Aw, Slim—"

"Aw, nothing, just do what I say."

"I *did* it already."

"Okay then." My mind is racing, making this up as I go along; anything to keep him from getting all frantic again. "Okay—now, first just take a little whiff of it, got that?"

"What's a whiff?"

"A *smell*, Isaiah. Just hold that bottle up to your nose and take a good smell, got that?"

Silence. Until—

"Phew! Mrs. Wise was right. It stinks!"

"Well, that's good. It's supposed to. That means it's strong, you see."

"Oh."

"Okay then. Now take a little dab of it on your index finger—your pointer, that's the one. Just a little dab now, you got it?"

"Got it."

"All right. Now, first you just do like you told me before, remember? Put that little bit behind your ears, where you feel that pulse beating—"

"Okay—"

" 'Cause that's where your own blood can soak it in, you see? Right through your skin."

"Okay."

"And that's gonna make you start feeling better in just a minute, you'll see."

"But it's not *me* that needs to feel better, it's—"

"I know, I know, it's your mama. I'm getting to her." Oh, Lord, what now? You got to scramble, brain. You got to think of something— "Okay, now listen to this. You just—just—"

"Just *what*, Slim? My neck is about broke, trying to hold up this phone while I do all this bottle stuff with my hands!"

"Well, you just—just put a little more on your finger," I say at last, desperate and clueless, "and you spell out her name with it, got that? *A-N-G-E-L-I-N-A*—right over your heart, on your skin."

"You mean under my shirt?"

"Well, of course, Isaiah, unless you're one of those dudes who wears your skin on the *outside* of your shirt—"

"Okay, okay, I get it. I'm doing it. *A-N-G-E-L-I-N-A.* Now what?"

"Now—now you have to concentrate, that's all. You have to picture every little thing about her—her eyes and her mouth, that star she wears on her cap. You have to hear the way she laughs, and think how her hands feel on your head when she checks whether you've got fever—"

"Okay—"

"You have to remember the sound of her voice when she's telling you a story, that mother kind of sound, you know?"

"Yeah—"

"And you have to taste all the good things she cooks for you, and remember how proud she looks when you do good in school, and see the way her skirts swirl out when she's dancing—"

"I can see 'em, Slim. I can see every bit!"

"And now you take all of those things together in your mind, and you—well, you just make 'em *stronger*, see? You say, 'Angelina Dodd, I'm taking the power of this Dragon's Blood, and I'm giving it to—' "

"Hold on, Slim, that's Aunt Alva coming out of—hold on just a—"

There's a loud *clunk!* in my ear that must be the sound of the phone dropping.

"Isaiah? Isaiah, what's going on? Are you all right?"

No answer but the distant babble of voices and the softer *clunk, clunk*ing that must be the receiver swinging against the wall.

"Isaiah! Isaiah, don't leave me hanging here like this! *Isaiah, come back, do you hear me?*"

"Slim?" It's Larry, coming down the hall. "What's wrong, honey? I thought I heard—"

"It's Isaiah. His mom's in the hospital. The baby's coming early, and—"

"Hey, Slim!"

"Isaiah? Is that you, Isaiah?"

"Sure, it's me, Slim. Who'dya think? But listen, I can't talk anymore. The baby's here—my sister's here—she's *all right*, Slim! My baby sister's all right, and Mama's doing real good. Aunt Alva says she's feeling better, and I can see her pretty soon. They're gonna let me go look at the baby in a minute, so I gotta go, Slim. Tell your dad and Mr. Casey for me, will you? Tell 'em everything's all right—"

"Sure, Isaiah," I say, smiling up at Larry as the phone goes dead in my hand. "Sure, I'll tell 'em."

✳

DAD STIRS a little when I whisper the good news in his ear.

"The baby's here?" he repeats hoarsely. "And Angelina—they're both all right?"

"They're fine, Dad. It sounds like they're doing just fine."

"Wonderful," he murmurs. "That's wonderful...." And then a shadow crosses his face, and he shakes his head. "But—"

"But what, Mack?" Larry asks. We're both leaning in, trying to catch his words.

Dad shakes his head. "The blanket," he says. "It's not ready yet—"

"It's okay, Daddy—" Through the sudden blur in my eyes I can just make out Larry, fumbling for a Kleenex on the bedside table. "You've already done the hard part—all the planning, remember? We can take it from here...."

23 ✳

THEY NAME the baby Halley.

"Like the comet," Isaiah tells me, smiling all over, smiles shooting out of his eyes and ears and *elbows* even, when Alva picks me up on Saturday and takes me over to the apartment to see everybody. "Because comets are made out of stardust, see? And Mama says that's where she's come from. Just look in her eyes! She's so new, it's hanging all over her still—little dusty bits of stars, see there?"

Well . . .

"Sure," I lie, not wanting to hurt anybody's feelings. I mean, how could I, with Angelina so happy?

"Isn't she beautiful?" she says.

And it's true, baby Halley's dark eyes *are* wondrous shiny ones, at that, even if so far the rest of her does sort of put you in mind of one of those little dried-apple dolls with the wrinkly faces. But a *cute* one, at least . . .

Anyhow I'm glad to get to see her finally. I love holding her downy head and squirmy little body close to my heart and—remembering those old kicks—thinking how strange it all is, having her out here with us now.

But I can only stay a minute; they might be needing me at home.

"You give your daddy our love, sweetheart," says Angelina, throwing me a kiss. "You tell him Halley says hello."

"Look how she's laughing!" Isaiah is saying as I start out the door. "Laughing in her sleep, and her so new. What's she got to laugh about, I wonder? What kind of dream could she be having, would make her laugh like that?"

"That's no dream," says Aunt Alva. "Just gas, that's all. Lots of babies do that way."

But Angelina is smiling. "Oh, I don't know. Maybe she knows something good. Some wonderful secret the rest of us have just forgotten, that's all."

And that Dad's only just now remembering? I wonder. Because even as bad as he's feeling now, every now and then his lips will twitch, and I'll swear he's laughing in *his* sleep, too.

"What, Mack?" Larry asks him once, when the laughing makes him cough. All three of us—Larry and Sister and me—are beside him this day, watching and worrying. "Is there something you need?"

The good eye opens just a fraction then, and even now I can see a glimmer there, a hint of the old sparkle. "Tell Buster to fix those pipes," he murmurs.

And then he's asleep again.

That's something else he and Halley have in common, come to think of it—all the sleeping, I mean. Like travelers resting up for—or from?—a trip. Does he know? I wonder. Is he awake behind those aching lids? Can he feel us here beside him?

It's been nearly four weeks now since our trip to the Hungry Valley, but I still think about it a lot. And sometimes I can't help wondering, if we hadn't gone, would he have had longer? Another few weeks, another month, maybe? Because it's true, no use pretending it's not, that trip wore him out. But here's the other side: it lifted him, too, when some deep part of him needed lifting more than anything. And in the end—well, what matters more? I don't know; you tell me. I suppose every person has to answer that question for himself sooner or later.

But I guess I know what my dad would say.

Anyhow I'm glad he had that day before the dying really started. Because after that it's not any fun for him; it's terrible is what it is. And as the days wear on, and more and more the only sound in the house is him fighting for breath, that terrible rasping breathing that won't let go and won't let go, sometimes I think I can't stand it another second. And then I want it to stop, I *pray* for it to stop, because it sounds like it hurts him so much. And at the same time I'm afraid every minute that it will. I'm terrified that it will. . . .

We're all with him when it happens—me and Larry and Sister—but Sister and I don't hear a thing. We've both dozed off for a minute, I guess—Sister on the rug and me at the foot of Dad's bed. When I wake up, Sister is still sleeping. And except for her gentle snoring, the room is quiet, quieter than any room has ever been, and Larry is holding Dad in his arms.

"Isn't he beautiful?" he says when he feels my eyes.

At first I don't understand. Where have I heard that before? I wonder. What can he mean?

Larry doesn't know himself, I guess, because what he

does next doesn't make any sense either. He lays Dad back down on the pillows and pulls the covers close around him, like he's afraid he'll catch cold. And then he stands up and walks to the closet, murmuring something about needing to find that crazy propeller hat Dad loves so much. "Rootie Kazootie," he's saying. "He'll want to have Rootie Kazootie. . . ."

"Larry?" I say, following him. "Larry, are you all right?"

But he doesn't hear me.

"Where is it?" he's saying now, pulling boxes and bags and old moth-eaten sweaters from the shelves. "You're such a mess, Mack. Just look at this mess, will you? I keep telling you you've got to get organized, don't I? Isn't that what I'm always saying?"

"Larry?" I try again. I'm getting scared now; I'm tugging on his sleeve. "Please, Larry—"

But he brushes me away—not roughly or anything, just like I'm a branch that's got him tangled up someway or a spider's web caught on his arm. "Where is it?" he keeps saying. "It has to be here somewhere—"

The closet floor is filling up now; he'll never find anything with the muddle he's making. He's pulled down an old green army coat and a scrapbook full of yellowed newspaper clippings and a crazy old clock with a statue of a guy bowling in the middle and a big gold trophy that says "It's Christmas Eve, Man!" on the plaque. He's got Dad's old tackle box that he uses for theatrical makeup opened and a jillion tangly fake mustaches and false noses and eyebrow pencils falling out. And then he makes the biggest mess of all; he tugs impatiently on what looks like the old Santa Claus beard, and that brings down a huge brown box with the word "Treasures" written on it in Dad's big careless

174

scrawl. And a whole other world of trash comes tumbling out of that—photos and hand puppets and the awful Crayola scribblings that I used to make when I was little, and—

"What in the—well, for pete's sake, Mack. This is the worst yet. What *is* all this glittery junk anyw—"

"My wings!" I cry out all at once, pushing past him into the closet and gathering the poor old feathery monstrosities into my arms.

"Wings?" Larry repeats, looking puzzled.

"Angel wings," I explain with sorrow, burying my face in their softness. "Big ones, you know, like they have—" And he's standing so still now that I have to go on, as if I'm teaching the alphabet to a small, slow child: "The wings you and Dad made for me, remember, Larry? That year in the Christmas play?"

It wakes him up somehow. "Wings," he says once more, but now he's looking at me like he knows me again, and his face is jagged with pain. "Oh, Slim. Oh, honey—"

And he reaches out to me, like a swimmer close to drowning, with the tears streaming down his face. And then I'm holding him someway; he's this big old bear man, but I'm holding him and rocking him and patting him on the back, like he's five years old or something. "It's okay, Larry, it's okay," I keep trying to say, except my voice isn't working right anymore. "It's okay, don't you see? Now he can fly. . . ."

24 ✳

WE'RE GOING back to the mountains today.

It's summer now, one of those warm windy mornings that you get around here sometimes in June, with the sun big and bright but not as hot as it looks, and those high-up wispy clouds, and the breeze blowing in from nowhere and everywhere, bringing sand from the desert and salt from the sea.

A good day for traveling, my dad would say.

I think he would have liked the memorial service. The celebration, I mean—that's what they called it: "A Celebration of the Life of Hugh Alan 'Mack' McGranahan the Third." A party is what it was, with all his friends. There must have been close to a million of 'em—Chesley and Leslie and Jenny and John and Connie and Jimmy and Helen and Bob and Roy and Michele and Paul and Art and Wes and Mel and Roxie and Ken and I don't know *who* all—not just praying the regular way but *their* way: laughing and crying and singing songs from Dad's old shows and telling his favorite stories.

Ms. Crofford was there, too, and everyone from the

group, and a planeload of friends and relatives all the way from Texas. And a couple I'd never seen before—a giant of a man in a string tie and his meek-looking little wife. "Mr. and Mrs. James Goode," he explained solemnly, shaking my hand. "We're real sorry for your loss, Miss Margery. Your dad was a prince of a fella. We all thought quite a bit of him over't the hospital."

No . . . Larry and I just looked at each other. It couldn't be, could it?

But it was—Jimbo and Old Woolly, in the flesh.

I think my dad would have loved that most of all.

My mom came, too. I didn't know how much I had missed her until I saw her face looking for mine when I met her at the airport gate.

"Hello, Mama," I said to her.

"Hello, baby," she answered.

And then she opened her arms, and that was all either one of us could manage for quite a while.

She's gone on back to Shreveport and Alex now, and as soon as school lets out next week I'll be going there, too. Not forever or anything—well, for most of the year, I guess, but I'll still be coming back to California sometimes for vacations and holidays. To our old house, you know, on the hill—Larry's and mine, and Sister's. And it'll still be here, I bet, no matter what kinds of fires or floods or mud slides L.A. has in store. I guess we can't do much about the earthquakes, but otherwise, between Larry and that ice plant, we ought to be pretty well covered.

I still wouldn't know what to call him if I had to fill out another one of those forms for school. *Friend* is true, but it's not enough.

He's my family, that's all I know.

There are just five of us making the trip today in the red Toyota: Larry and me and Isaiah and Angelina and sweet little baby Halley. And Sister, too—I guess that makes six.

Or seven, if you count Dad. But he doesn't take up much space; he's just a bagful of ashes inside a white box, sitting tight in my lap right now.

There's no fog today, thank goodness.

"Think we'll see Mrs. Wise again?" asks Isaiah as the first peaks loom into view.

I shake my head. "I called to make reservations, but Buster said they were closed for the month, heading up to Lake Tahoe to play the slots. I just caught him going out the door. But I told you that already, remember? That's why we're taking the picnic."

"Oh, yeah," says Isaiah. "Hear that, Halley? It's your first picnic, how about that?"

I'll swear, he's so goofy over that baby, I'm afraid he's starting that—what do you call it?—second childhood. Before he ever got the first one done.

We pull into the Hungry Valley in record time.

"Would you look at that?" says Larry, checking his watch to see if it's still ticking. "An hour and fifteen minutes flat. Amazing how easy it is when it's easy!"

"But the flowers are gone," says Isaiah. "I wanted Halley to see the flowers!"

"She'll see them next year, and all the years after," says Angelina, and she looks off peacefully into the dusty brown hills, like *she's* seeing them already.

Will Angelina be here, too, I wonder, for all those springs to come?

BE HERE FOR THE CURE—that's what the posters say, trying to tell people to get tested. And maybe she will; maybe she'll make it long enough for the scientists to figure this thing out. Maybe one day we'll have that victory bonfire Ms. Crofford talked about. I hope so anyway.

And meanwhile—well, I'm through sitting on my rear end, that's all I know. I'll do *something* over there in Shreveport, or wherever the microchips take us; I'll march in parades or write letters or baby-sit cats or, I don't know, stand on my head, but I'll do *something*. It may not be much—it won't bring my dad back—but like Suzannah says, it beats the heck out of *nothing*.

I keep thinking about those monkeys, you see. The thing that bothers me about them is they're not really *gone* at the end of the movie. They're not even tame, exactly. Sure, they're glad their crabby old boss has melted—who wouldn't be? I mean, face it, she couldn't have been all that much fun to work for. But the way I see it, those monkeys aren't really good or bad, either one, by themselves; they're just dumb animals. It's *who their boss is* that makes all the difference. And that's what makes them so dangerous, see? Because they'll follow anybody—witches, wizards, whoever gets there first. So you can't ever just forget about them and think, Oh, great, now we can relax, at least we've clipped their monkey wings. Because they're still *around*, and if you don't keep your eye on 'em, there's no telling what else they'll do.

Or who they'll be following next.

Larry's packed a great lunch, of course—maybe not quite the feast we had last time we were here, but a ton of good stuff: four kinds of sandwiches on homemade bread and his special vegetable dip and pickles and radishes and those good potato chips and chocolate-chip cookies and Milk-Bones, for Sister. And we spread it all out in a nice little flat spot down under the Face and eat until we can't eat any more.

And then we sit there quietly for a while, thinking about my dad.

Wishing he were here.

But he is here, after all. That's why we've come.

"Are you ready, honey?" Larry asks me when a little more time has passed.

"I guess so," I say. And then I go and get the white box from the car, and for a few minutes we all just stand around staring at it, trying to think what's the right way to do this thing.

"Would you like to say something?" Larry asks me now.

But I look at Sister looking at me with that puzzled, mournful expression that she's worn for the last three weeks, and I shake my head. There's too much to say, and nothing at all.

I can't fit my dad into words.

And I guess Larry feels the same way, because he nods a little and pats my shoulder. Then the two of us take off the lid and open the bag inside, and holding Dad between us, we start scattering him all around while Angelina and Isaiah—with the baby in his arms—stand back a little, watching.

And then a funny thing happens.

I guess we should have thought about the wind. It's been blowing on us all day, not bothering anybody but just *moving*, you know? Whipping the hair in our eyes and rustling in the tall brown grass and cooling the sweat off everybody's brow just enough so that after we ate, Angelina wrapped little Halley in Dad's blanket—which I finished up yesterday, like I promised him I would.

Anyway all of a sudden that wind picks up again. Just as we're shaking the last of Dad out of the bag, it comes dancing right at us out of nowhere and everywhere. And the next thing we know we've got ashes all over—not just on the ground and filling the air, but in our eyes and mouths and up our noses and covering our hair and clothes—in us and around us and through us. And at first we all just *look* at one another, kind of panicky, you know? Thinking, Oh, no, what a mess. This isn't the way it's supposed to be—

Until Sister starts to sneeze.

That does it. Pretty soon we're *all* sneezing; we're sneezing and coughing and laughing all at once, with the tears running down our cheeks.

"Oh, Lord, oh, Mack," Larry keeps saying, shaking his head and wiping his eyes with the grayest handkerchief I ever saw. "You never *would* leave a party, would you?"

And it seems right somehow, better than anything we could have planned, after all—that Dad wouldn't stay put, like a regular person. That part of him will be going home with us—and to the dry cleaners and down our bathtub drains, I suspect; he'd have loved that, wouldn't he? Sure he would; I can hear him laughing now. And part will be riding the wind. And part will be staying right here in the Valley—for what Mrs. Wise calls the show.

Stardust, I guess you could say.

Baby Halley starts to fuss a little.

"Let me hold her for a minute?" I ask Isaiah.

He hesitates, but his mother nods, so he sighs and hands her over. "Watch her head, now," he says.

"*I* know," I tell him, taking the little squirmer in my arms.

"She's wishing for the flowers," he says.

"Oh, Halley," I say, "don't cry, little girl. Just you wait. There'll be gold and green and even chartreuse and . . ."

"All the colors of the rainbow," Larry finishes when I can't.

Halley isn't listening. She screws up her funny little dried-apple face and waves her fists like a tiny prizefighter.

"You don't believe me?" I ask her.

Larry smiles. "Everyone's a critic," he says, putting his arm around me.

But I'm not giving up. I wrap Halley tight in her one-of-a-kind blanket and hold her close to my heart. "Just you wait, Thomasina. Just you wait."

✳

Special thanks to:
  Kevin, Michael, Brian, and Errol Cooney
  Richard Jackson
  Ricky Carlson
  Barbara Crofford and The Los Angeles Shanti
    Foundation
  Uncle Jim Nelson
  Sheila and Art Tybor
  Joe Cooney and Karl Dutt
  Dylan and Becky Gelke Baker
  David Doty
  Glenn Holtzman
  Mitch Mitchell
  Richard Roberts
  Ronn Carroll
  Timothy Arrington
  Hilary and Clare Fields
  John Barker
  Mr. and Mrs. Lloyd Hamilton
  Susann Fletcher
  Thommie Walsh
  Randy Hugill
  Michael McAssey
  The Reverend Tom Miller
  Terry Pierce
  Leslie Uggams
  Tom Flagg
  Lynn Mitchell
  Linda Crew
  Mike O'Rourke

Tom Joslin and Mark Massi of *Silverlake Life:*
The View from Here
All Saints AIDS Service Center, Pasadena, California
AIDS Project Los Angeles
Being Alive, People With HIV/AIDS Action
Coalition, Los Angeles
Project Inform, San Francisco
KAIROS Support for Caregivers, San Francisco
Maggie Herold and everyone at Orchard Books
Anne Tobias

AND REMEMBERING ALWAYS:
Thomas Hulsey
Brick Hartney
Tommy Rogers
Steve Leatherwood
Greg Murphy
Steve Marland
Nat Santoro
Ricardo Ramos